CRAPPED OUT

A Novel by
John Anthony Moccia

Stark House Press • Eureka California

CRAPPED OUT

Published by Stark House Press
1315 H Street
Eureka, CA 95501, USA
griffinskye3@sbcglobal.net
www.starkhousepress.com

CRAPPED OUT copyright © 2023 by John Anthony Moccia. All rights reserved, including the right of reproduction in whole or in part in any form. Published by Stark House Press by arrangement with the author.

ISBN: 979-8-88601-011-4

Cover design by Steven Ray Austin, enigma media, Austin TX
Book design by Mark Shepard, shepgraphics.com
Proofreading by Bill Kelly

PUBLISHER'S NOTE:
This is a work of fiction. Names, characters, places and incidents are either the products of the author's imagination or used fictionally, and any resemblance to actual persons, living or dead, events or locales, is entirely coincidental.
Without limiting the rights under copyright reserved above, no part of this publication may be reproduced, stored, or introduced into a retrieval system or transmitted in any form or by any means (electronic, mechanical, photocopying, recording or otherwise) without the prior written permission of both the copyright owner and the above publisher of the book.

First Stark House Press Edition: January 2023

Lots of federal agents retire to Florida. Jack would have preferred to have been killed in the line of duty rather than face this decline. He was incapable of having his mood brightened by the eternal cheeriness of the staff at the Sunny Laurel Senior Living facility. These people had no idea who he was or what he'd done and he wasn't about to tell them.

They didn't care that he and his colleagues were largely responsible for cleaning up a corrupt nation—that they had risked their lives daily on dangerous streets meant nothing to either the caregivers or his fellow residents. That he and his colleagues had gathered evidence and hunted down treacherous killers and ruthless thugs was meaningless to people who only seemed to care if you finished your dinner and took a good crap.

They all acted as if they were dealing with a brain-addled geriatric. He might be cranky but his brain was just fine. At least he was pretty sure it was fine...

Dedication

To Joan Marie
Proof Reader, Tech Advisor and Wife of Infinite Faith

Chapter 1

Jack Hannigan sat in his La-Z-Boy in the living room of his tiny studio apartment. He had his feet up. In this position the 78-year-old, with his brush cut white hair and his lanky six-foot two-inch frame, looked reasonably fit. The picture of health. Stand him up and his slouch revealed the cracks.

He stared at the mantelpiece of his never-used fireplace. On one side were three pictures of a woman who appeared to be of his vintage. On the other, propped in temporary positions were a picture of thirty-year-old Jack wearing a dark suit with a small gold badge pinned to his lapel. The picture was bordered on the right by an American flag. On the left was a blue flag bearing the gold and silver seal of the Federal Bureau of Investigation. Two other frames featured impressive citations signed by former FBI Director William Webster.

Jack's right hand was wrapped around the stock of a 9 mm semiautomatic pistol. A bath towel was draped over the back of his chair. He took a deep breath, tightening his grip on the weapon.

There was a knock on his door and a woman's voice called out, "Mr. Hannigan?"

"Dammit," he whispered.

The knocking persisted. "Mr. Hannigan, are you in?"

He shook his head and tucked the gun under the seat cushion.

"Mr. Hannigan?"

"Jesus Christ. *What?*"

"It's Sally Woznecky. I need to ask you a question. Are you home?"

He put his hands on both arms of the chair and, with some difficulty, pushed himself into a standing position unsure what hurt the most, his feet, his knees, his back or his hips. Pain was telegraphed in that order. He went first to the mantle and flipped over the pictures of his law enforcement past. Then he limped toward the door and opened it, keeping the chain on the lock.

Outside stood a short, plump pleasant-looking woman in her forties. She wore a blue smock with a name tag and a big smile.

"Hi, Mr. Hannigan. Top of the morning!"

"You had a question?"

"You weren't at breakfast."

"That's a statement, not a question."
"I was wondering if everything was okay."
"Yes. Peachy," he started to close the door.
"You weren't hungry?"
"No. Apparently not."
"Have you been regular?"
"Regular at what?"
"Your bowel movements."
His eyes narrowed.
She gave him a bright smile. "We need that fiber, Mr. Hannigan. All of us do."
"And how was your bowel movement today?" he asked.
"Great and I'll tell you why."
"That's okay." He began to shut the door, but she continued.
"Are you excited?"
"About what?"
"Your new neighbor across the hall. He's moving in today."
"What happened to my old neighbor?"
"Mrs. Tinker? Sadly, she left us two weeks ago Friday."
That meant she had died. Hannigan's expression indicated he didn't really care. "Oh, well."
"But I think you'll be liking the new fellow."
"Why?"
"He reminds me a little of you. I mean personality-wise."
"As long as he's not a rapper and doesn't blast hip hop music, it doesn't matter."
She chuckled. "Oh, no. I don't think we have to worry there."
"Okay. Anything else?"
"Lunch is in an hour."
"Oh, boy."
"Corned beef today."
"Yay. Thanks for stopping by." He closed the door before she could launch into another topic. She had broken his mood—not improved it—just killed the train of thought.

Chapter 2

Two hours later the elevator dinged at the end of the hall. An old man, Bill Smith, rolled out in a wheelchair. He was so obese that the chair strained to bear his weight. He wore dark glasses and a sour expression. Accompanying him was Sally Woznecky and a tall attractive brunette in her early thirties. This was Bill's daughter, Maria. Sally, with her eternal smile, pointed down the hall.

A roll of fat pushed out on each side and also the back of Mr. Smith's chair. Despite his age, which was eighty-one, he had a good head of jet-black hair, combed straight back. He wore a baby blue polo shirt, tailored slacks and polished loafers.

From his apartment Jack had heard the elevator's arrival and struggled upright.

"Bet you're thrilled, Mr. Smith," Sally declared.

"About what?"

"Your new apartment."

"No."

"C'mon, Papa," the girl gently urged. "Let's give it a chance."

Smith dismissed the idea with a wave of his hand. "I was being honest. I'm not thrilled."

They arrived at his unit, directly across the hall from Jack's. Sally unlocked the door and pushed it open with a flourish. "Ta-da. Welcome home, Mr. Smith!"

Smith fixed his position in the hallway, barely looking inside. "This ain't my home."

"It won't take long before you'll feel like it is," Sally persisted.

Jack finally managed to get to his door and pressed his eye against the tiny peephole. His view was limited to the backs of three heads as Smith's daughter pushed her father across the threshold. Then the door shut behind the new arrivals.

Inside the apartment, Sally swung around with arms outstretched like she thought she was Vanna White flipping letters. "Maria spent all last week decorating it for you. You'll love the pictures and mementos she brought here."

He looked at his daughter, softening. "You did this?"

"I want you to be comfortable."

He gave a Mediterranean shrug. "It don't matter."

"Listen," Sally said, "I'll let you get settled. Dinner is in about an hour and a half. Maria, you're welcome to join your Dad for his first meal here. We're having pot roast tonight and it's yummy. See you later." She headed for the door.

"Wait!" Smith called. "Let Maria leave now if you're locking us down."

Sally laughed. "Why would we lock you in, Mr. Smith? There's your key on the nightstand. You come and go when you wish."

Smith seemed a little surprised by this but only repeated his dismissive shrug.

Sally headed out to the hall and down to the elevator as Smith studied his new surroundings.

"So what do you think, Daddy?"

"About what?"

"Oh my God! About what? Your new place?"

A frontal view of father and daughter suggested that they did not belong to the same genetic strain, or even the same class. Maria was tall, slender, casually but tastefully dressed and she displayed the sort of, well, elegant innocence of a young lady who had been sheltered from all distress, and privately educated—maybe at a convent school. Smith, though also expensively dressed, looked more like an off-duty longshoreman who had bought his outfit at the pro shop of a golf club to which he did not belong. Maria spoke without accent, without pretense, and with a certain shy articulation. Smith's tone was guttural and harsh—urban ethnic, like he was from the south side of some place big.

"What's to think? It's a freaking old folks' home. Am I supposed to jump up and down?"

"You have to admit, it beats your last one."

He squinched his lips. "You think? So far, I ain't so sure."

"You're impossible. Look, you have a living room, a little kitchen and an almost separate bedroom. Your own toilet!"

"Oh, boy." He got out of the wheelchair and hobbled toward the window. "Not much of a view."

"There are trees and look, a pretty blue jay. Wow! Look at the blue jay, daddy."

"That's supposed to cheer me up? You treat me like I'm the Birdman of Alcatraz. Maybe it's you that's getting senile." He hobbled back to his wheelchair and practically fell in.

She looked defeated. "You can still come back and live with me. Remember?"

"How you gonna find a husband with an old man living in your house?"

"I'm not looking for a husband."

"If your mother heard you say that ..." He shook his head. "They shoulda just let me die where I was."

She turned the wheelchair around and got on her knees taking his hands. "Will you stop? You have to give this place a chance! If you don't like it after a week, I'm bringing you to my place. We'll get a good home care nurse. Better than the last one. Fair?"

Across the hall Jack grew bored looking at the closed door through his peephole. He retreated to his La-Z-Boy and spun it around so that he was facing out his own window, staring at a tree. This is how he spent most of his day. He watched the same squirrel he had watched every day for weeks. The squirrel stared back, then jumped to another branch, showing off his agility.

Jack half-smiled, then raised and shook his fist at the squirrel. He didn't begrudge the animal its freedom. He would admit to no one that he actually enjoyed the animal's company. He had even named him (or her). He was afraid that made him sound more than a little crazy so he kept that secret even to himself. Merle, that was the squirrel's name. Male or female, it worked.

Then he sat back in the chair trying to get his mind to return to the level of conviction he had held before that repulsive Woznecky woman had interrupted him. He fished the handgun out from under the cushion. At that point Merle the Squirrel jumped up to his window sill and stared at him like he was a loser. Jack sighed. His original mood was now irretrievably broken.

Chapter 3

Lots of federal agents retire to Florida. They are no more immune to dementia and the ravages of age than the rest of the general population. They are no less prone to living in their glory days than others of equal years but are perhaps a tad less tolerant of the fact that the younger generation has labeled them with a past-due date. They tend to be hypersensitive to dismissal by their juniors. At least that's how it was for Jack.

To have lost a spouse and to be isolated from former colleagues then thrust into an environment where his only interaction was with diaper-wearing neighbors, was all the more painful. Aside from facility staff, his only contact with a vital, healthy, stable person was with his son, who Jack believed considered him to be little more than an obligation.

He would have preferred to have been killed in the line of duty rather than face this decline. He was incapable of having his mood brightened by the eternal cheeriness of the staff at the Sunny Laurel Senior Living facility. These people had no idea who he was or what he'd done and he wasn't about to tell them. They wouldn't have a clue what it had been like. As far as they were concerned, he might as well have worked in a frigging grocery store or had a rug cleaning business.

They didn't care that he and his colleagues were largely responsible for cleaning up a corrupt nation—that they had risked their lives daily on dangerous streets meant nothing to either the caregivers or his fellow residents. That he and his colleagues had gathered evidence and hunted down treacherous killers and ruthless thugs was meaningless to people who only seemed to care if you finished your dinner and took a good crap. Don't even mention the fact that you had to spend your meals sitting across from a bunch of drooling literal hairbags!

He half-wished that the small portion of his brain that was still capable of thought would quickly die like those sad bastards that were locked up in the memory care wing—a place that would more logically be called the no-care wing, where he could actually become as invisible to himself as he had become to the rest of the world. The truth of it was that life was only worth living if you had hope. You only had hope if you still had something to accomplish and you only had something to accomplish if you had a project to keep you busy.

He had no project. If he was going to have one it wouldn't be stupid bingo.

No. He intended to take one step beyond the memory care ward. He was going for death, which at this point sounded pretty good. There'd been no other reason for him to keep his old Glock. He had been smart enough not to mention it to anyone when his kid moved him into this place. It wasn't as if he needed protection in here. If anyone had spotted his piece, they probably would have taken it away. Go ahead and try, he would have said. "Out of my cold dead hands!" Christ, he sounded like one of those right-wing survivalist gun nuts, which he wasn't. He was just a seventy-eight-year-old that no one remembered and no one else cared enough about to ask.

Jack was willing to concede that he had become perpetually cranky but he felt his crankiness was justified given the way he was treated by those around him. Bottom line: he did not appreciate that the best response he was able to evoke from people he encountered was gentle solicitousness. They all acted as if they were dealing with a brain-addled geriatric. He might be cranky but his brain was just fine. At least he was pretty sure it was fine.

Chapter 4

Though each unit in the facility had a kitchenette, full meals at Sunny Laurel were universally taken in the communal dining room. Residents were not encouraged to cook in their apartments since management did its best to avoid the obvious liability that poorly supervised stovetops engendered. It was not uncommon for residents to heat up a meal over a cooker and then forget about the process until the smoke alarms blasted.

The dining room was home to fifteen tables set for six, a beautiful fireplace which was never lit (this being Orlando) and a long buffet where ambulatory residents served themselves breakfast. Seating was assigned. In making these assignments much thought was given to the compatibility of the diverse diners. Making seating assignments was an inexact science since internecine feuds were frequent and reassignment was often necessary.

Both the men and the women preferred same-sex seating arrangements. To seat the men and the women together historically had proven to be a bad idea.

Dinner, served between 4:30 and 5:30, generated the greatest attendance. Maybe this was because beer and wine were served, upon request, during this meal. Or maybe it was because, by this time of day, most of their complicated toilet issues were, as best could be, resolved.

At dinner, for alcohol-based beverages, two was the maximum. Again, this was a liability issue. For those who desired to drink in excess, or perhaps to at least enjoy a pre- or post-meal cocktail, they were free to keep their bottles of choice in their own apartments.

At the men's tables, what with the beer and wine, nascent fantasies were fueled. For whatever reason it was not uncommon for some of them to adopt dramatic pasts which were pure fiction.

Jack Hannigan was assigned to a table now consisting of only four residents. If he were to classify the group in which he was thrust it would belong to a category he would describe as Near Senile-Liberal. Perhaps Jack's assignment was made in error because of his son's employment. In Jack's view he was neither liberal nor especially conservative. His previous employment required a non-partisan stance. Of the original six at his table, one had recently died and another had progressed from Near-Senile to Full-Blown. The man had been quietly moved to the memory care unit never to be seen again. He was not missed since he had a habit of removing his dentures mid-meal and dropping them into his water glass for a quick rinse. The dead guy's departure was not mourned either since his hygiene in recent weeks had deteriorated to the level that his tablemates believed he might have died days before he actually stopped breathing.

When a new person was assigned, he usually faced a mild interrogation which was limited to three questions: "Where are you from and what did you formerly do?" and "Who did you vote for?" The latter questions were meant to establish if he was friend or foe.

It was not uncommon for a new resident to feel he had been stripped of all dignity and therefore to assign himself a more dramatic persona to salvage his damaged pride. At certain tables those who had served in the military, however briefly or however unvaliantly, often wore ball caps labeling themselves as veterans of specific wars: WWII, Korea and/or Viet Nam. That few of them had personally experienced combat did not mean they didn't claim fighting experience. All expected to be thanked for their service even if, in truth, their service had been minimal or definitively safe. More than a couple of them had invented other new professions with the hope that they didn't run into actual members of those new professions. Some might allege to be doctors or lawyers—even actors. Often they claimed careers as industry magnates, but the dullest among them on the conservative side veered toward make-believe macho professions such as CIA, Navy SEALS, Green Berets, or as former carrier pilots, and SWAT team members. Whatever they had actually done, all had earned reasonably well since otherwise they could not have afforded residence in Sunny Laurel which had a basic cost of $6000 per month.

While it could be argued that Jack Hannigan was perhaps one of the few who had retired from a dramatic profession, he had learned long before his entry into assisted living that it was smartest to not let anyone but his closest friends know what he had actually done for a living. It should also be noted that his closest friends were also members of law enforcement. Tell an outsider that you had been an FBI agent and you were doomed to eternity hearing stupid theories about the best ways to enforce the law. These theories were as prevalent and as useful as belly buttons. When asked, he was either intentionally vague or he posed as a member of an innocuous profession which killed extended questioning. As far as anyone at his table knew, Jack had sold insurance. No one thought enough of this occupation to inquire further. Mostly, the general male population at his facility considered it much more important to tell you about their imaginary pasts rather than to learn about yours.

The three at his table were Irwin Schlotzy, who claimed to own a department store chain in Connecticut and to have founded an orphanage in Africa on the side. His most prominent characteristic was extreme flatulence. It was manifested as both resoundingly audible and unimaginably olfactory—at times so strong as to make the eyes of any one in proximity water. For his sins, Irwin expressed no apology. His standard response? "Whatsa matter? Don't look at me."

Morris Chalmers asserted that he was a philanthropist. Jack doubted if his philanthropy extended beyond modest annual office contribution to the United Way.

Then there was Fred Winter, who claimed to be the retired talent agent who discovered Lady Gaga, or at least someone named Lady GooGoo, since this was the client he most often bragged to have represented. He also claimed to have discovered the legendary actress Elizabeth Tuller, whoever the hell she was.

"What happened to the butter?" Jack asked one evening as he looked for the dairy product to garnish his bread.

"I haven't seen it," replied Chalmers as he slurped his tomato soup.

"You claimed to own an insurance company," Schlotzy snidely responded. "Why don't you file a claim?"

"Yeah? Why don't you quit farting? I didn't say I *owned* an insurance company," Jack declared. "I said I was in insurance. By the way, if somebody tried to take out a policy on you, it would be denied. At your current rate of farting you'll be deflated in a week!"

"Did Schlotzy pass gas?" Morris Chalmers inquired.

"What? Are you, deaf?"

"I suppose I am a little."

"Doesn't your nose work?"

"It doesn't, now that you ask. Taste and smell seem to have gone the way of my sex drive."

"Then let's trade seats."

"I'll stay put, thank you. If I stand, I won't be able to sit again."

"Yank on your schlong," Winter suggested. "It will make your knees flex. That's a line I stole from Milton Burrell. Happiest days in my life was when I got that Uncle Miltie show on the Comedy Channel."

"Really?" Jack asked. "I think Berle was dead at least 20 years before the Comedy Channel even existed."

"Shows how much you know."

"Sweet Mother of God," Jack said quietly to himself. He wondered if he might escape these village idiots if he asked for a transfer to another table.

As ill-tempered as he was, Jack Hannigan was by no means the most mean-spirited member of the flock. Tablemates took turns vying for the title of Mr. Irascible. If an argument became too serious—if, for example, the verbal combatants began to reach for the dinnerware in manners that could be deemed unnecessarily aggressive, then prompt table reassignment was imperative.

Tonight, Jack's table was down to three members. Less was better as far as he was concerned.

Schlotzy, the guy next to him, between flatulent outbursts, sucked on a strip of beef thoughtfully. "Do either of you guys have any idea what it's like to have to get up and take six pisses in the middle of the night?"

"Usually," Jack said, "I try to take just one at a time."

Winter shook his head. "Try not being able to take a crap for five days. Do you know what that's like?"

Hannigan laid down his fork and looked exasperated. "What do you think it's like listening to this conversation about your bathroom habits when I'm trying to eat dinner?"

Chalmers snorted. "Probably about as pleasant as trying to soothe my digestion when you're always on the edge of a temper tantrum."

Chapter 5

Bill Smith was admitted to Sunny Laurel following a couple of serious falls at the home of his daughter, the recently divorced art gallery director Maria Dooley. Mr. Smith needed a little more looking after than Maria was able to provide given that her job required her to be gone most of the day and included some travel.

He had Type A Diabetes, and was about two-thirds blind. Of growing concern was the fact that he was experiencing a significant loss of balance.

The first step for Ms. Dooley had been to hire a live-in caretaker, an older woman from Nigeria who had been a nurse in her country of origin. This did not work out since Mr. Smith suggested she had apparently become a thief in her adopted country. Never proven. What was proven was that Mrs. Nkote, a widow, was as strong-willed as her patient. She was not about to take any unpleasantness from the old man whatever she was paid. It was, by no definition, a therapeutic relationship.

"So, Dad. I just don't want to see you unconscious on the floor all by yourself."

"I would prefer to die on the floor by myself rather than listen to that screaming pain in the ass order me around all day."

"I'll find another caretaker."

"No. You won't."

"Then I'll quit my job. I think we can afford it."

"No, you won't. Forget it."

"Assisted living?"

"No way."

"You need somebody here with you."

"Screw that. I can take care of myself. In fact, I'm here to take care of you. I just want to be left alone."

Maria placed some brochures on the tray table of his wheelchair.

"What are these?"

"Doesn't that place look nice?"

"It looks like phony bullshit. One of those old folks' homes, where they take your money and poison you."

"It's called senior living. You have your own apartment. You eat what are described as gourmet meals served in a dining room or they deliver the food to your apartment. Staff will check on you regularly but they respect your privacy and only intrude if there's an indication of a medical emergency. It's just a couple of miles away from here. I'll be able to see you pretty much as often as I do now, but you will have your own place."

"I'm not going. I'll move out on the street where I won't bother nobody."

"You are not bothering anyone now. I'm sorry, I won't let my father move out on the street."

"What's it cost?"

"You can afford it."

"I'm not calling them."

"You don't have to, I have an appointment for us tomorrow there. They've even invited us to lunch so that you can sample their cooking."

"Tomorrow I'm watching the Phillies-Nationals game."

"That'll be a first. You hate baseball."

"I'm taking an interest."

"We'll record it."

"Before that I need a ride to the sporting goods store in the mall."

"What for?"

"I need to buy my tent for when I move out to the street."

"We can probably get you a good one at that military surplus store near Disney World."

"Good."

"We'll stop there after our lunch appointment at Sunny Laurel."

"Promise?"

They never bought the tent. Following the Sunny Laurel tour and lunch and the conversation-interview with Sally Woznecky, Smith reluctantly agreed to give Sunny Laurel a one-month trial. He made it clear to all within hearing range that he was doing so just to make life easier for his daughter. This move would be made under protest and, he declared, he wasn't about to take any shit from nobody.

Maria Dooley gave Sally an apologetic look. Sally gave her a wink to indicate that she got a kick out of recalcitrant old men. In fact, they were her specialty.

Smith, for his part, decided that he wanted things the way they used to be, before he ended up in Maria's home, but he was smart enough to realize that he would be hoping for too much to dream about the days when he was still married and lived in the big house up north where he had about fifty people he could call upon for anything, day or night. That was great but would never happen again. No, he'd settle for that other assisted living "home" where he lived until Maria talked him in to coming home with her. He never thought he would admit it but he even missed that place.

Chapter 6

The phone by Jack's bed rang. He immediately began the slow process of lifting himself from his chair. There were four rings before he made it to his nightstand and grabbed the receiver.

"Agent Hannigan."

The caller chuckled. "Agent?"

Jack shook his head. "Habit. What's up Mikey?"

"Dad, I prefer Michael."

Jack smirked. "Michael sounds more like some kind of an interior decorator."

"Or a successful young lawyer. Which I am. You named me."

"Successful? Define successful. Your mother named you, kid. I was in favor of Mack even Max, but it sounded too Kraut. What's up?"

"I have to cancel Sunday."

"No problem."

"Yeah, I need to go to a barbecue at my supervisor's home. Kind of a command performance."

"Yeah, okay. Have fun."

"You miss one of these things, they don't say anything, but they're keeping score."

Jack shook his head and glanced at a picture on his bureau of a tall young man in a cap and gown.

"Yeah, no problem. I was thinking of grabbing a beer with some of the guys."

"What guys?"

"Just some old timers from the Bureau. Guys who moved down to this hellhole of a state when they pulled the pin. They're always calling, you know?"

"How will you get there?"

"One of 'em will swing by."

"Which one?"

"Probably Kohanski."

"I thought he died."

"Well, one of 'em."

"Remember. No more than one beer."

"Yeah, yeah."

"So, how you been doing?" Michael inquired. "You taking your meds?"

"Hey, I gotta go. Someone's at the door."

"At your door? Who?"

"Probably one of the women on the floor. They drive me nuts."

"Yeah, okay. I'll call you tomorrow."

"Okay."

Jack hung up. He felt relief more than regret. Mikey was a good kid but he wasn't visiting because he wanted to. Hannigan knew this. The boy was doing it out of obligation and, truth be told, the visits were painful for both of them.

So Sunday would be just another day, sitting around hoping Merle would climb the rotting pine tree. Unless.... He reached under the cushion of his easy chair and studied his service weapon. It might be a good day for a shooting.

Jack's nose began to twitch. He was smelling something bad. His eyes narrowed as he shuffled toward his door. He opened it and sniffed the hallway. Then he crouched and went across the hall to his new neighbor's door and sniffed again.

He straightened, limped back to his apartment and slammed the door. Dammit! He went to his phone and dialed a single digit.

A cheerful voice answered. "This is Sally."

"Yeah. I thought there was no smoking in this place."

"Oh, hi. Is this Mr. Hannigan?"

"Yeah. I'm making a complaint."

"By all means, what's wrong, Mr. Hannigan?"

"This new ass ... the new guy across the hall is smoking a cigar in his room and it's stinking up the whole place."

"Oh, my. A cigar?"

"Either that or he died already and expelled some extreme gas. He's breaking the rules and I don't care for it."

"Of course. I'll take care of it immediately. He's new and he may not be familiar with the house rules yet."

"Yeah? Well get him familiar, or I will." Hannigan hung up.

A few minutes later Jack stood over his toilet trying to beat the odds of numerous nighttime sleep interruptions when he heard footsteps in the hall and a big knock on his new neighbor's door.

Smith waddled to his doorway on a walker. He didn't say much as Sally politely explained the No Smoking policy to him. He just listened, staring at her through his dark glasses.

Then he said, "That makes no sense. No frigging sense. It's a little late to be worrying about my lungs."

"It's not that, Mr. Smith. I'm sorry to say that a neighbor has complained."

"Which neighbor?"

He caught her making an involuntary glance at Jack's door. "It doesn't matter. Our smoking policy is very strictly enforced."

Smith glared at Jack's door and said, "Yeah, all right."

"Thank you. I appreciate your cooperation. And don't forget tonight's Bingo Night."

"Yippee." A word which had never been expressed with less enthusiasm.

"Five o'clock sharp! Mrs. Winnow won $15 last week."

Smith shook his head, swung his walker in reverse and kicked his door shut. He retreated into his living room, steaming as Sally headed to the elevator.

Jack smiled with satisfaction and headed back to the toilet. A minute later he heard a banging on his own door. The banging continued.

"Hold your horses! I'm coming."

"Yeah, well hurry up, dead nuts!"

Jack's eyes widened. It had been a while since he had heard such language. He struggled with his zipper, flushed his toilet and began to navigate his way across his living room rug.

"I'm gonna say it once," Smith growled through the door from the hallway. "You got any complaints, you tell me personally. Don't go running to no gash."

By the time Jack reached for his doorknob his neighbor's door slammed shut. The hall was empty.

Jack stepped back, shut his own door but his eyes were wide. He stumbled over to his chair, hyperventilating. He shook his head like an unconscious man trying to wake himself up. It took him a full minute to calm down.

"The *hell?*"

He got up opened his door and hobbled across the hall. He banged on the door with the same force Smith used on his.

"Hey," he shouted. "Get out here!"

"Screw yourself, I'm taking a leak."

"Who do you think you are?"

"Nunna your goddamn business. Get lost, you know what's good for you."

"Yeah? Well be careful, pal." As he considered waiting it occurred to him that he hadn't finished his own leak. He had also not finished pulling up his zipper. He swung around and sauntered, to the extent he was capable, back to his apartment slamming the door.

Chapter 7

Jack sat in his chair, stewing. No way. No way was he in the mood to let this new jerk slide. Jack might be getting old, maybe even a tad infirm, but this guy had to know who he was playing with. He put on a cardigan, not noticing that he'd missed a hole in the buttoning process, causing the sweater to sit in a pronouncedly lopsided fashion on his long, slightly hunched back. He threw open his front door and marched to the elevator.

When his son had first moved him in three months earlier, they'd made such a big deal about the two-story place having an elevator. He swore to all present he didn't need an elevator. He'd take the stairs just like he had always done at the Federal Building to his office, seven floors up. The only time he took the elevator was when he had a prisoner in tow.

He managed, on the first day of his residence at Sunny Laurel, to get up the one flight to his apartment. It had taken nearly five minutes to complete the journey then another ten to try to figure out if he was going to puke or pass out. When he got inside his room he chose the former and decided that—strictly in the interest of time management—the elevator in the future might not be a horrible idea.

After his unneighborly confrontation, at a quick clip—relatively speaking—he made it to the elevator bank and poked the down button.

In the lobby, he looked around and was pleased for a change to see Sally Woznecky at her desk in the lobby. She'd be an easy source.

"Why Mr. Hannigan, we don't get to see you down here often enough."

"Breakfast, lunch and dinner isn't often enough?"

"Not for me. What can I do for you, dear?"

"What time did you say Bingo was tonight?"

"Five o'clock. Do you expect to play?"

"Probably not."

"I'll save a couple of cards for you, just in case. I promise you they'll be lucky ones."

"Oh, boy."

"Did you get a chance to meet your new neighbor yet?"

"Kind of." This woman just walked right into his ruse. He hadn't lost it yet. "But what'd you say the guy's name was?"
"I don't believe I mentioned his name. He's a sweety isn't he?"
"Yeah. That's what he is. Mr. Uh ..."
"Smith. Yes. I knew from the beginning you two would get along."
"I forget where he said he was from."
"I'm afraid I've forgotten as well."
"Remind me, again. What's his name?"
"Smith, Mr. William Smith."
"Ah, Smith. Common spelling?"
"The only way I know how. Listen, I have a suggestion. Perhaps you should consider inviting him to join you at Bingo. That might be a nice way to break the ice and get a chance to know him. Make him feel welcome in his new home."
"Dumbest idea I ever heard." He swung around abruptly, or somewhat abruptly, and headed back toward the elevator bank.

Sally showed a slight raise of alarm with her eyebrows, then shrugged. "Don't forget," Sally called. "Five o'clock sharp for Bingo. You don't want to miss even the first game."

"Yeah, yeah, yeah."
"Marge is tonight's caller."
He turned around, puzzled. "Marge?"
"She's hilarious."
"Can't wait."

Chapter 8

Smith's daughter sat in his room facing her dad.
"Papa, why do you look so upset? Are you in pain?"
"Yeah, I got a pain. A pain in the ass and he lives across the hall."
"You don't like your neighbor?"
"He's a *gidrool!*"
"A *gidrool?* He's a cucumber?"
"You know what I mean."
"What did he do?"
"I smoked a cigar. One of my last pleasures. And this clown rats me out to Admin."
"Those things do smell kind of foul, Dad."
"You get used to 'em, believe me."
"Mama never did."
"God rest her soul. She was a sensitive one, your mother. Sometimes too sensitive."
"Well, you don't want to hear this but maybe this man did you a favor. The last thing your lungs and your heart need right now is smoke. If you want, I can get you some nicotine gum."
"Screw that."
"Dad, look it's a beautiful day outside. Why don't we go out and sit in the sun?"
"You want to go out to the yard?"
"Here they call it a garden."

Maria pushed her father's wheelchair from the lobby to the garden. There were paths that wove in and out, statues, an artificial waterfall, and a small dock by an artificial pond.
"Isn't this beautiful?"
"Did you bring my smokes?"
"Uh, no."
"No problem," he winked. He pulled half a stogie from his shirt pocket and lit up.
"Better."
"You're killing yourself."
"I'm just helping along what God already wants."

Michael sits with his father on a bench at the other end of the garden. They are having equally bad luck in dreaming up small talk. Jack sniffs the air.

"What's that smell?"

"What smell?"

"It's coming from over there." He pointed to the waterfall. "Do you see anything?"

"I see kind of a pretty girl."

Jack stood up and peered over the hedge. "That's got to be him. I'll bet he's that fat s.o.b.!"

"Who, Dad?"

"That new jerk across the hall. The guy with the cigars. He's smoking out here now. He is breaking the law. You're not allowed to smoke, period. Call Management."

"Actually, Dad, he's not breaking any laws or rules right now. He's allowed to smoke outside."

"Like hell. And do you know what he said to me earlier?"

"No."

"Let me get a look at the guy." Jack stood, probably too quickly, and started toward the hedge. He began to teeter.

Michael jumped up quickly and caught his father before he dropped and eased him back to the bench. It took a number of breaths and a full minute before the fainting spell passed.

"By God, I intend to confront him."

"The older gentleman with the pretty caretaker? Why? Let him enjoy his walk in peace."

"Like fun! You should've heard what he said to me. He's got no idea who he insulted."

"Let me get you inside. You almost passed out. Let me get you some water. You need some rest."

"Who does he think he is?"

"Okay, Dad. Are you able to stand? Let's get inside."

Jack glared but didn't budge.

As they passed the waterfall. Maria took her father's arm as he hobbled along on his walker. "Papa, do you know that man back there?"

Anthony glanced over his shoulder. "Yeah he's a piece of … He's a clown."

"You don't know that."

"I know that!"
"And that young man with him. Is that his son?"
"Probably. He looks like a clown, too."
"From here he looks kind of handsome."
"You've been with enough freaking Irishman to last you a lifetime. Stay away from him."
"How do you know he's Irish?"
"I can smell 'em."
"I think he's kind of cute. He was looking over here."
"Flip him off. No? I will."
"Daddy!"

"Hey, Mikey. You got a camera in that telephone?"
"My cell? Yeah, they all have cameras. Even the one I just got you. Why?"
"Can you make it zoom?"
"Sure."
"I want a picture right now of that dumb-ass waterfall. Let me see how close you can make it get."
"Don't you want me to wait until those people move?"
"No. Do it right now. Quick."
"Okay, relax." He pointed the phone toward the water feature, hit the zoom button and clicked. "Okay, now what?"
"Take a few. I want to see how clear they are."
"Oh, believe me. The camera feature on these iPhones is excellent."
"Take a few."
Click, click, click.
"Great. Now show me."
Michael switched over to the gallery file and held the phone up for his father to see.
"Hey, not bad!" But not great. He could now add one more field that his son showed no particular talent in, photography, but at least he got the shots and they were somewhat decipherable.
"I told you."
"Just great. Can you print them?"
"I can forward them to your email on your computer. But look. The guy you think you hate is in the way. He kind of ruins the view of the waterfall. But I like the looks of that girl, don't you?"
"Meh."

"I tell you what, Dad. Get to know that guy and maybe I can meet the daughter, what do you think?"

"I'd think that maybe at least you're not a fag."

"Do you think I'm gay?"

"I wonder sometimes, you know? I mean you're what, forty?"

"Try thirty-two."

"Most guys, by the time they're thirty-two have been married twice already. How many times have you been married?"

"As you know, zero."

"How many grandchildren have you given me?"

"Again, as you know, none."

"So you see what I'm saying?"

"You wanted me to go to college, right?"

"Sure."

"Then you insisted no less than a thousand times while I was an undergraduate that I go law school."

"I just didn't want you to become an AIDS-ridden junkie."

"Well, mission accomplished. And now I'm a lawyer. Isn't that what you wanted?"

"It was because you didn't seem quite cut out to join the Navy SEALS. Now if you could just use that degree and maybe get somewhere in the government instead of being, what, some kind of sob sister?"

"Dad, I'm an associate in an internationally respected agency."

"Doing what, defending criminals?"

"I'm defending freedom and liberty. Is that something to be ashamed of?"

"Yeah, it is."

Michael opened his hands preparing to give a fuller explanation but before he could launch, Jack cut him off. "I think I'm ready for my nap, now."

Michael breathed a sigh of relief. "I'll walk you back to your apartment."

"Did you send me those pictures?"

"Uh, yeah," thinking he had just witnessed one more example of his father's mental decline.

Michael Hannigan took after his mother. Sort of. More to the point, he did not take after his father and this was the cause of their conflict. Michael was a worrier. He spent his days worrying about his job performance, his legal cases and the fact that he had not yet fallen in love with a woman. Mostly though he worried about his father. That his Dad was depressed was no secret and, consequently, it depressed Michael—in spades. He had hoped that when he got Jack into Sunny Laurel his father might develop new interests, maybe even a love interest—the assisted living facility was full of widows—and more than a few seemed to have their eyes out for a new mate. But even suggest such a thing to his father and the old man looked like he'd take a smack at you. This look was actually a staple of Michael's childhood.

In fairness, Michael hadn't been an abused child, not in the conventional sense. His father had never actually struck him. He just had a way of looking disappointed whenever his only child expressed his independent aspirations. It felt worse than a smack.

It seemed that none of *his* dreams fit his father's dreams for him and Jack Hannigan was unable to adopt the philosophy that he would be happy if his kid did whatever he wanted as long as he did his best. Honestly, his default reaction appeared to be anger when he was unable to get Michael to adopt Jack's own personal goals. It was more disappointment than anger but the impact was the same.

You see, Jack Hannigan was very proud of what he had achieved. First, that he had been selected as a Special Agent in the FBI and, later, that he was promoted to the rank of supervisor. It had been his dream since he was ten years old and he wanted the same for Michael. As it turned out, it wasn't Michael's dream and this had been difficult for Jack to accept. Michael's lack of approval from his father had not been enough to steer him away from doing what he wanted. It was enough though, to permanently affect their relationship.

Now, after so many years, their roles had been reversed. Michael worried constantly about his father's well-being. He knew how miserable his father seemed—unmoored—not just without goals but completely without purpose. He derived pleasure from nothing. He had no one with whom to commiserate. No hobbies. No interest in books. No like-minded friends. Michael stayed up nights trying to think of ways in which his father could achieve pleasure. The old man hardly even drank any more.

Michael even considered showing his dad how to look up porn sites on the Internet. But Michael had spent too many years at

Catholic schools being harangued by nuns to feel good about that move. Besides, his dad would probably have a heart attack if he suggested it. Rigid was too fluid a word for old Jack Hannigan. The man was seemingly incapable of veering off the path of righteousness toward anything that normal people might consider enriching. He was the quintessential stereotype. He never dallied. When the man was sworn in as a Special Agent of the Federal Bureau of Investigation, he was *sworn in*. He was the iconic straight arrow. For him, even having an evil thought, was a step in the wrong direction.

As a father, Jack had been involved to the extent that his job and his limited emotional range permitted. But his involvement was mostly characterized by fear and caution. On the job he saw so many examples of what could go wrong with a person, that he was overly protective. His biggest fear was that Michael would make a mistake, innocent or otherwise, that would ultimately haunt him. Jack's definition of the ultimate haunt could be summed up by worrying that his son would become involved in any activity which could cause him to fail a background investigation. An error in judgment by Michael might not only ruin the boy's future prospects, it could even harm Jack's career.

In retrospect, perhaps Jack's biggest mistake was that he had always assumed that Michael would want to follow his path. He believed that his kid, like him, would choose a life of service in law enforcement or maybe even the intelligence field. If Michael chose not to join the FBI, fine. Jack would accept his son if he decided in favor of a career in the CIA. He'd even be proud if the kid became a prosecutor. If Michael was rejected pursuing any of these choices, Jack would settle for his son seeking a commission as an officer in a branch of the military. In the event worse came to worst, as a last choice, Jack would settle for Michael selecting a career in one of the lesser federal law enforcement agencies.

Whatever his path, it was essential that the boy's reputation remain unblemished. He had to avoid all the pitfalls that tripped up almost any normal teenager. There would never be a valid justification for youthful experimentation with alcohol. Don't even mention drugs. As important, he had to stringently avoid association with kids who chose to dabble in either of these pastimes. Lie down with dogs and you come up with fleas, was the mantra the father expected his son to live by. Jack secretly ran criminal records checks on the families of the kid's known companions.

Whether he wanted to or not, Michael should try out for organized sports. He needed to show his capability as a team player who was willing to take the occasional thumping. It mattered not at all that Michael preferred books to scrimmages. Jack did not seem averse to the concept of Michael becoming involved in legal activities that might be physically dangerous. Dangerous activities—rock climbing, alpine skiing, sky diving—so long as they were legal and built character. This concept went untested since Michael again had little interest in such activities

The final result was that never once had Michael shown the slightest interest in either law enforcement, the military or intelligence work. For him, these fields offered the scent neither of romance nor glamour. By observing his father and his father's associates, though he would never mention this, he had a pretty good idea how truly unexciting such a career could be. Worse he saw what being a Federal agent had done to his father. Michael could never personally become fixated beyond reason in the hunt to destroy a criminal organization, nor did he believe he was capable of the other upward paths that an agent could pursue.

When it came to fighting crime, his father could be diagnosed as obsessive compulsive. His goal was to bring every member of an assigned Mafia family to justice.

No thanks, dude. It was rolling a boulder up a hill as far as Michael was concerned. Whack-a-mole. Take down a target and another popped up, one after the other until you were mandatorily retired at age fifty-seven. While the retirement package was generous it did not include what Michael considered should have been required: a therapeutic deprogramming-decompression regimen. Older agents were left holding their dicks in one hand and a loaded gun in the other. Maybe the Bureau needed to open its own assisted living facility, an approved pasture where special agents could go to feed on the comfort of their shared experiences.

Cops and agents spent their careers progressively self-isolating. The deeper they got in their fields the more they tended to associate only with each other. They developed a hardened conviction that no one else was like them. Everyone else was boring and not worth conversing with.

For Jack Hannigan in particular, retirement was not an easy

transition. He had tossed around the idea of joining some of his old colleagues in private investigations and corporate security, but then his wife got sick and Jack devoted his life to her care. By the time that tragedy ended, it was too late and he was too unconnected to venture into something new.

Michael was away at school during most of the period of his mother's decline and only caught glimpses of the effect her poor health was having on his father. He wasn't there to witness Jack's foundering disorientation after the man had lost both his career and the only woman he had ever loved. It felt as if everything he had earlier gained had been wrenched away. There had been no one there to help find new friends or new interests. He was without an anchor.

In spite of pretending otherwise Jack had no network of former colleagues. He briefly considered staying in the suburbs of Philadelphia to be around the people who were part of his life but, for very good reasons, not a lot of people remain in Philadelphia beyond their careers. There were virtually no colleagues left up there. So he went to Florida where his son went to law school and where Jack was a stranger to his new community. He had no connections. The warmer weather offered no solace. He had nothing to do but go downhill. Jack Hannigan was not a golfer. He was not a fisherman. He didn't even like to eat fish and the only time he did so was on Fridays, because he had to. He sure as hell wasn't a bridge player or a sun bather. All he could do was decline.

The only bright spot on the horizon for Jack was the fact that it appeared that Michael, upon undergraduate college completion, appeared to have kept his options open. He was admitted to law school. Jack prayed this would lead the kid to one of the earlier discussed fields. Michael was smart enough not to share with his father his secret and that was he dreamed of becoming a lawyer who specialized in the preservation of human rights. He joined the freaking American Civil Liberties Union.

If you had anything on the ball when you got out of law school, things went uphill rather than down. The days got harder. Michael struggled long hours to find a place in the ACLU. He worked ten or twelve hours a day to keep on top of his cases—cases which he found interesting but excruciating. He knew better than to discuss his job with his father. He would get the same reception if he told the old man he had become a pedophile. Jack Hannigan's position was that humans already had too damn many rights and the only ones requiring reform were the damn criminals themselves. The closest Michael knew that he could get to his father accepting him would be if the old man fell so deeply into dementia that he forgot his own name. They were not near that milestone yet, so instead Michael Hannigan was obsessed with developing for his Dad a diversion that might move him beyond his terminal depression. His father's mental decline was occurring, but at glacial speed. Early signs showed no indication that his symptoms would include a joy factor.

Though his contacts with his Dad offered neither a sense of mutual fulfillment nor even unilateral reward, Michael tried not to miss one of his twice-a-week phone calls or weekly visits. His attitude during these meetings could be summed up in a word: resignation. The same went for the old man. The best he could get from Jack was a litany of complaints about Sunny Laurel. Idiots, according to Jack, surrounded him here.

If you looked hard enough for credit to bestow, at least Jack was not a whiner. He didn't want to burden his son, so he internalized rather than verbalized most of his complaints, but they became no less obvious to Michael. Somehow, though neither of them could define the benefit, they both needed to maintain their contact.

Still, though it might not be readily apparent, Jack dearly loved his son. Michael was all that he had left to love. Was he disappointed in how the young man had turned out? Absolutely. But he had gotten to the point that he could almost acknowledge that the kid could have turned out worse.

Michael didn't begrudge his father who he understood had always wanted the best for him. He just understood that the two had very different measures for what was the best, even though one had driven the other.

Jack was the straightest of arrows. He harbored no secret life. Michael knew this. He was neither proud nor ashamed of that fact. Michael himself had demonstrated no delinquent proclivities. But if he followed his father's rule of law, wasn't he in violation simply for associating with the rest of humanity?

For many years it was smothering. Now that he was thirty-two years old, it was something of a relief to see that his father was losing it. Jack could no longer control Michael if he couldn't control himself. Michael now toyed with the idea of rebellion knowing that his father was no longer in a position to dictate his behavior. Maybe he'd even grow that beard, or at least a small goatee. He thought about that a lot.

Chapter 9

Jack was back in his room and he was upset. A father might not be able to expect much from his son but what he always should be able to expect was that his son would adopt and be willing to carry on the feuds of his father. It was the Irish Code for chrissakes!

He had pointed out the jerk across the hall to Mikey, that fat-assed puddle of lard. A normal kid, back in the day, would have nodded and said "Let me deal with him, Dad." But Mikey wasn't a normal kid, oh no! He was all for liberty and freedom of expression. It was time he accepted that. What he did instead was tell Jack to calm down. Told him he shouldn't rush to judgment and he should give the guy a break. To hell with that! Jack Hannigan had been paid to make judgments and he was pretty good at it, too But did the kid back him up? Like fun.

Jack was sure he had beat that slob back upstairs and he would wait behind his peephole to get a good straight-on look at him. Then he'd throw open the door and confront him. "Hey, hotshot, what did you call me? You want to say something, say it to my face and see how long it takes me to knock you to the floor!"

A couple of minutes later he heard the ding of the elevator and sure enough, who arrives in his wheelchair but Fatso. Unfortunately, he was being pushed down the hall by that tall girl, who—Jack had to agree with Mikey for a change—wasn't half bad. He couldn't exactly jump through the door and demand that the clown apologize in front of this young woman. He'd better wait until he caught the guy alone.

As the girl fumbled with the old man's key Jack had an opportunity to get a half-good close-up look at the man. Jesus, from here the guy vaguely looked like somebody. Maybe Jack needed to get his eyes checked again, get new glasses. But dammit, the resemblance was close. So close he caught his breath and got a little dizzy again.

He needed to sit down. This just couldn't be. He grabbed the arm of his La-Z-Boy and slid down. NO! Just the thought made him consider he might be getting a little senile. He shook his head. He wouldn't even allow his brain to express the guy's name. To do so would confirm he was going nuts.

Chapter 10

It might not have been that significant. Okay, so Jack had a dream about the guy he thought Smith looked like. After all, he'd spent a good part of his career dreaming about that guy—watching him during the day—dreaming about him at night. Jack could be a little obsessive that way. Well, maybe he didn't personally watch him in the day, his team did. Basically, they were the ones on the street. From the comfort of his office, Jack would study the still shots of the slimeball and then the videos and then listen to the recordings that came up on the wire. But it *felt* like he had lived with the guy. He was in front of Jack day and night.

If he were honest, Jack actually saw him in person a grand total of just a handful of times. From his car, it was always at a distance. The last time was in the courtroom. He could have watched the full trial and have seen him in person for about fifteen days, because the trial lasted about three weeks, but to do so would have been to show interest in a case that turned out not to be his. The deadbeat accountants at the IRS had scooped the Bureau. The FBI was one piece of evidence short, maybe a month away from sealing the case and the U.S. Attorney had said screw them and had gone with the Revenue nerds. Ah God, how that still hurt.

So Jack had sat in the back of the courtroom for only one afternoon to watch as his guys testified to a few sexy details before the tax boys bored everyone to death with flow charts and balance sheets. He wasn't about to honor them with his attendance. But that day in court when he decided to show up as a spectator, he never took his eyes off Mr. Fat Ass, wondering if he was going to break his chair.

What was it now? How much time had passed? Something like eighteen years. No way this guy across the hall could be the same guy. Jack pushed his chicken around his plate over dinner, pretending he couldn't hear the people at his table while he was waiting to see if Fat Blob the Neighbor would make an appearance. Usually Jack was in and out, eating and running, not even faking being polite with his tablemates.

Then lo and behold, in the slob limped, using his walker. Roll, thump, roll, thump until he landed three tables east. The guy was as big as a house, or at least as wide as one. He managed, from entrance to seating, to make eye contact with no one. He was here to conquer one thing: food. He had no social interest.

Jack stared at him. He stared at the guy hard. His size was the same. The hair was mostly the same. He looked much older than the man Jack remembered, but hell, eighteen years would do that to you.

Hell, if it wasn't him, it was his twin. But get serious! *It could not be*. It was just another obese geriatric. Fatsos tended to look alike once they passed seventy and this guy was definitely past seventy. He called himself "Smith" which was a bit too obvious for an alias. Besides, he'd only taken his fall eighteen years ago. Jack did the math. Under those Federal Sentencing Guidelines, it was too early for him to be out. Even if they gave him all the good time in the world, it wasn't enough. Jack's guy would still be in the can. Even if he weren't, what were the chances he'd end up in Orlando? And then, how the hell could he possibly end up in the same assisted living dump? There was, in a nutshell, no chance at all. None.

Jack felt a little scared. No one liked to think that they were going nuts. He stared at his plate trying to get up the strength to stand and go back to his room. Maybe he'd just look at the stupid squirrel for an hour before the *Evening News* came on.

He took a breath and looked up. Was the guy looking at him now? Hard to say with those silly-ass shades on. Guy probably couldn't see the plate in front of him.

Chapter 11

Smith stared at his plate of spaghetti through his sunglasses. He sighed deeply then looked across the room and glared. He wasn't glaring at Jack Hannigan. He could not even specifically see Jack Hannigan and if he did, he wouldn't recognize the guy. He couldn't even see the old bastards who sat at his own table across from him. Smith was pissed—pissed at that ugly little gash, Sally What's-Her-Name.

Tonight's menu offered the choice of roast chicken or spaghetti. Smith ordered the spaghetti. What could go wrong? But this crap? Chopped up spaghetti noodles smothered in some kind of red sauce which he would bet came out of a jar by Chef Boyardee or some gook. Then they mashed it up and spread around some hamburger on top. It was sacrilege!

He intended to have some words with Little Miss Sally to set her ass straight.

"Hey," he growled at his tablemate, a gay retired librarian.

"Yes?"

"You see that little broad Sally out there?"

"Why, no. I don't think so. Who is she?"

"Motheragod."

Forget it. There was something bigger bothering him. Bill Smith knew he was being watched. Without looking around he could feel the person's eyes on him. That was a skill he had developed decades ago. Staring wasn't polite. In certain settings it meant someone was after you. In certain settings it meant someone was planning on killing you. In those same settings, if you returned the stare, it meant you had to kill him.

He looked up from his plate and saw several tables away a shadow that appeared to be looking in his direction. It brought up the obvious question. Why?

Hey, maybe it was the clown who lived across the hall that ratted him out for the cigar. Yeah, that was it. Fuck him. If the guy wanted to take it further Bill Smith would handle him. Your move, pally.

Jack did his best to forget about it. He still had enough circulation in his brain to realize he should be more concerned about his own mental health than to be thinking that the guy across the hall was the same guy he had devoted the latter part of his career trying to nail—a guy who got thirty-five years hard time could not have turned up as a new resident here.

Jack would not dare mention his suspicion to anyone, not even to his own son. To even suggest such a thing was to demand a more intense level of care. They would probably put him on a heavy regimen of drugs for starters and then start asking him if he needed help taking a shower or lowering himself on the can. It would only get worse.

The best course of action to take was to forget the whole thing. It was just a figment. No way. When the thought started crawling back to him he would block it, just like the priests used to tell him how to block any thought that might involve naked girls. He had gotten pretty good at that.

It was a simple exercise. When a prohibited thought began to enter his mind, he would first shout—to himself, of course—"No, get out! I'm not interested!" And then he would mentally change the subject to something more wholesome, like a banana split or something. It worked, most of the time.

It was strictly by accident that he happened to be heading to the can to take like his nineteenth leak of the morning when he heard the elevator ding. It was only a minor detour which he should have resisted but he headed instead to his door and his peephole.

Then from the hallway he heard the roll, thump, roll, thump of "Smith" heading toward his apartment. Jack was perfectly placed for the best vantage point yet and here he came. What a fat sonofabitch. Wait, what was he seeing on the right side of the guy's neck? No!

Jack had forgotten a lot of things, but oddly, his training kicked in. What he always seemed to remember: the most pronounced physical characteristics of a suspect. In the case of the crumb across the hall, aside from his obesity—his most pronounced physical characteristic—was the one-inch mole just to the right of his Adam's apple. Tell me, what are the chances of that also being a coincidence. Right! There was no chance at all.

He was looking at the neck of freaking Anthony Finelli! Yep, Anthony Finelli, former crew chief of the Nicky Scarfo mob that had run Philadelphia and Atlantic City! He didn't know how it was possible but it was him. Confirmed.

Chapter 12

He probably should have checked in with the Orlando Field Office months ago when he first got down here. He should have given them at least a courtesy call to let them know he was here and available if they needed him for something. He was still willing to act as a resource if they needed an expert on La Cosa Nostra stuff. Locally, he was probably one of the few guys that knew anything about the LCN. But he hadn't called because he'd had a lot on his plate. The Orlando guys probably knew he was here—surely they knew his reputation—but didn't want to bother him just yet until he settled in.

Jack studied the telephone directory. Telephone books were mostly no longer printed. Many of the residents at Sunny Laurel weren't comfortable searching for numbers online so the staff of Sunny Laurel made sure each room had a book by the phone, even though the book was sorely out of date. But a hard copy was important for the comfort of their guests. Jack found what he was looking for in the Government Section and dialed the number. One ring and a female receptionist responded.

"FBI."

"Yes, can you connect me with the duty agent, please?"

"Stand by, sir."

A second later a male voice came on the line. "Special Agent Walsh."

"Yes, this is Supervisory Special Agent Jack Hannigan."

"I'm sorry, who?"

Jack repeated himself, then added, "I'm with the Philly Office."

"What can I do for you, sir?"

"I need you to trace a name for me."

"Trace a name?"

"Yeah. I just need his location."

"Supervisory Special Agent Hannigan, you said. I'm sorry, I don't recognize ..."

"I'm retired."

"From this office?"

"No! I told you, I was up in Philly."

"Philadelphia, Pennsylvania?"

"I see you know your geography." Jack was starting to sound agitated.

"But you're in Florida now."

"Yeah. It happens."

"Where in Florida?"

"Here. Orlando."

"May I ask your address and phone number."

"I'm in a retirement … I'm retired."

"Yes. You said that. What's your address, sir?"

"Sunny Laurel. I forget the street."

"It's okay, sir." The tone switched to a more kindly one when the agent began to understand he might be talking to someone who wasn't all there.

"Yeah. I need you to locate a guy I used to handle. Anthony Finelli. Ring a bell?"

"Not really. No."

"He's a mob guy. With the Scarfos."

"The who?"

"The Scarfo Family. LCN. They used to run Philly and AC."

"Atlantic City."

"Now you've got it. This crumb has been in prison since about 2003."

"Uh-huh."

"I think he's here."

"Here?"

"At Sunny Laurel."

"Looking for you?"

"No. I mean I don't know. He's living here. Across the hall."

"Ah, that must be upsetting."

"Listen, bud. He's supposed to be in prison. Federal prison."

"They all get out sometime, sir."

"I know they all get out sometime, okay? But this guy got thirty-five years. I'd call 2021 a tad early, wouldn't you? Unless they've changed the sentencing guidelines."

"And it's mighty coincidental that he ends up across the hall, isn't it?"

"Okay, you think I'm nuts, right?"

"It just seems unlikely."

"9/11 seemed unlikely too, didn't it? You're not going to look into it?"

"I'm not saying that, sir. I'm just saying that … well …" The guy was looking for a reason to cut the conversation short. "We'd need more than what you have so far to pursue this."

"Just get on your computer and figure out which joint he's supposed to be in and see if he's still there, then call me back. How hard is that?"

"I can't give this information to a civilian."

"I'm not a civilian."

"You're retired, sir. I'm sorry. I'll need something more concrete than that the person across the hall looks a lot like somebody you used to know. Is there anything else I can help you with?"

"Listen, son. This one's got a mole on the right side of his neck. I remember that mole."

"Sorry, sir. Maybe you should take a little walk, get outside and get some sun. I'm sure you'll feel better."

Jack slammed down the phone.

He sat in front of his desktop studying the pictures Mikey had forwarded. The guy he was sure was Finelli could have been any obese blob. In the e-mailed images the neck mole was invisible. If you want something done right, you have to do it yourself. How many times had he learned that lesson?

Jack dialed his son at work and reached his secretary. "American Civil Liberties Union."

Jesus. Every time he heard it, he wanted to puke. "Can I speak with Mikey, uh, Michael Hannigan?"

"May I ask who's calling?"

"His father."

"Oh, how nice. One minute please."

It was more like five minutes. At least it felt like that. Finally, "Dad?"

"Yeah, hey Mikey."

"*Michael*. Is everything all right?"

"Yeah, sure. I need you to pick me up something."

"Dad, I'm in a meeting."

"When you get out."

"Sure. What do you need?"

"I need a tube of graphite and some Scotch tape."

"You need what?"

"A tube of graphite and Scotch tape."

"Uh, okay. What in the world for?"

"Ah, you know …"

"I don't know, to be honest."

"My key gets stuck in the door."

"Your key."

"Yes. My key. It gets stuck, okay?"

"I'm sure the maintenance department at the facility can help you."

"Just get me a damn tube of graphite and some tape, okay? I'm working on something."

"Yeah, sure, Dad. I need to get back to the meeting. I have to go now."

Chapter 13

The following Saturday Michael and Jack are sitting on their usual bench in the garden.

"Have you had any more contact with your new neighbor?"

"He's a lowlife. Do you know who he really is?"

"Um, no," Michael said immediately regretting having raised the topic. "Who?"

"Never mind." He knew if he told Mikey who he thought it was, the kid would call a shrink or something.

"Who?"

"Forget about it."

"Okay, but you brought it up."

"No I didn't!"

"I didn't. You did."

"No *you* did."

"Whatever. Just forget about it."

"Okay. I forgot about it."

"You think I'm nuts?"

"Um, no. But sometimes you *do* sound a little crazy when you get mad like this for no reason." Michael struggled to find a way to change the subject. "By the way, I brought that tube of graphite and Scotch tape you asked for last week and the tape."

"Let's have it."

Michael fished the items out of his pocket and Jack snatched them out of his hand.

"Well, thanks, Mikey. Great visit. See you next week." He turned quickly and raced, to the extent that he could race, back toward the entrance of the building.

"Dad, wait a minute. Where are you going?" He caught up with him.

"I have to get ready for lunch. Tuna salad today."

"I don't believe you. What's wrong, Dad?"

"Um, I have to go to the bathroom."

"Oh, uh, well. Let me walk you back to your room."

"No need, son. See you next time. Thanks for stopping by."

Mikey watched as his father made it through the front door. He shrugged and whispered, "Bye, Dad" and turned toward the parking lot.

Chapter 14

Jack got off the elevator and hustled, sort of, down the hallway. He looked around to make sure that no one was close. He extracted the tube of graphite, uncapped it and carefully sprayed a thin layer on Anthony's doorknob. Then he whipped around, after secreting the tube in his pocket, and entered his own apartment.

That night, when he was sure that Anthony and everyone else was fast asleep, he snuck across the hall with two wide pieces of clear tape attached to the sleeve of his pajama top. He pasted one piece of tape to Anthony's doorknob then carefully removed it. When he got back inside his own living room, with minute care, he removed the tape and carefully stuck the sticky side against a clear piece of broken glass, making sure not to smear the surface of the first tape. Perfect. Then he grinned at his handiwork. "You still got it, kid."

Chapter 15

Jack sat on a bench outside the front entrance to Sunny Laurel. Sally had just parked her car in a staff space and approached him cheerfully.

"Mr. Hannigan? Are you waiting for someone?"
"Nope. I'm just sitting here."
"You look like you're waiting."
"I've got a taxi coming."
"A taxi? Our shuttle driver will be happy to take you. Are you going shopping?"
"Nah. Just a routine doctor's appointment."
"We can get you there. No need to pay a taxi."
A cab pulled to the curb.
"Whup, here he is. Nice talking to you."
The driver hopped out and opened the back door.
"Well, please be careful," Sally said.
"Yeah, yeah, yeah." He gave Sally a dismissive wave.

Jack limped into the FBI Office. The receptionist eyed him with concern from behind the bulletproof glass. Before he made it to the window she leaned toward her little microphone and spoke, not at all unkindly. "Sir, the VA clinic is the next floor down."
"Thank you. I'm not looking for the VA Clinic. I'd like to speak with Special Agent Walsh. I didn't catch his first name."
"Did you have an appointment?"
"He's expecting me."
"But no appointment?"
Jack fished in his jacket for his credentials. Across the narrative portion was superimposed a stamp in red which said "Retired". "I'm Supervisory Special Agent Jack Hannigan."
"Retired," she added as she studied his offering.
"Yes, retired. But I spoke with Walsh a few days ago about a matter and said I'd get back to him."
At this FBI office—maybe every FBI office in the country—they were accustomed to odd visitors, many downright crazy, showing up daily. Most of the offices have an interview room just off their lobby, located there conveniently to quickly speak with and dispose

of pests. In fact, whenever a nutcase walked into any of the multiple other Federal law enforcement agencies to explain how they were receiving clandestine messages and radio signals through their hair follicles or their fillings the other agencies took joy in sending the person directly to the FBI. The other agencies did this because they were pretty sure that the Bureau had nothing better to do.

"I will tell him you're here."

"Thank you."

"Please have a seat, sir."

That was better.

A full ten minutes later Agent Walsh stuck his head out the door of the interview room. He looked like he was not too many years out of high school. A Freakin' New Guy. Actually, put him in a white short-sleeved shirt, a skinny black tie with a little black plastic name placard over his pocket, maybe give him a bicycle, and he would have looked very much like one of those Mormon missionaries that used to annoy the hell out of Hannigan in the old neighborhood.

Maybe Jack was being unfair. The kid had probably completed graduate school. He at least had a four-year degree and the short haircut might have been a holdover from time spent as a young officer in the military. If so, he probably had a deployment or three to Iraq or Afghanistan under his belt. Whatever. The onset of puberty wasn't, for Agent Walsh, that far in the rearview mirror.

Walsh looked slightly annoyed. The secretary pointed to Jack sitting in the lobby. He only dropped the annoyed façade after the secretary gave him a warning look. He offered Jack a slight wave before he pointed to the interview room. "Mr. uh, you asked to see me?"

"Agent Walsh?"

"Yes, that's me."

"Jack Hannigan. We spoke a few days ago. You were going to look into something if I could provide further information."

Walsh struggled with his memory. "Hannigan? Oh, yeah. Aren't you the old … uh, former agent—?"

"Supervisory Special Agent. Retired," Jack pulled his retired credentials from his pocket, flipped them open and laid them on the desk that separated the two.

Walsh picked up the creds and studied them.

"This is you?" the young man grinned.

"Who the hell does it look like? It's an old picture."

"I'll say. It looks like it was taken about 1920."

"They teach you history? The Bureau was not established until 1935."

"No, I know. I was just saying, it's an old picture."

"I'm an old agent."

"You said you were in New York, or was it Newark?"

"I said Philadelphia."

"That's right! Foreign counterintelligence?"

"No, the Organized Crime Squad. LCN."

"Organized crime. In Philly. That must have been some assignment. Those Italians were kind of violent back then weren't they?"

"Under Nicky Scarfo and Philip Testa, it was the most violent family in the U.S."

"Interesting." His tone indicated that it wasn't particularly.

"Do you remember who I was calling you about?"

"Let's see. Some old *goombah* named Finestre, right?"

"Finelli. Anthony Finelli."

"That's it! I was close."

"Not close enough to get it right. So did you do any checking?"

"What year did you retire?"

"2007."

"Okay. Yeah I did check on your guy and he got, what thirty-five years in the can in about 2006 on an IRS beef?"

"In 2003. That's right. They piggy-backed their case off of ours."

"They do that. And now it's 2021."

"Yep."

"Which is almost eighteen years ago."

"Almost, but not quite. Under the Sentencing Guidelines, he's not due out until maybe around 2032, with good time. That's when he's due, but he's out right now and living right next door to me."

Walsh gave him a look of sympathy, pretty sure about who he was dealing with. "Uh-huh. Well, like I told you on the phone. Without further proof, we can't really do anything. Look, Mr. Hannigan, lots of old white guys look alike. Sooo, listen, it's been really nice talking to you, but we're very busy in this office and ..."

"I've got further proof."

The young agent didn't hide his eye roll very well. "You do?"

Jack fished in his pocket and pulled out a plastic cup which held the broken glass with the fingerprint tape attached.

"What's this?" Walsh asked.

"What's it look like?"

"It looks like one of those cups they give you to pee in at the doctor's office."

"That's just the container. Inside you'll find tape that holds a very neat fingerprint specimen."

"Belonging to?"

"Anthony Finelli. From his doorknob across the hall."

"So you're saying he's escaped from the U.S. Penitentiary at Lewisburg."

"I'm just saying he's out. I don't know how."

"Yes, well, I'm afraid there's not much we can do with that."

"Bullshit. You have a fingerprint tech here don't you?"

"Well, yeah."

"So all you have to do is download Finelli's prints and do a comparison."

"You don't understand."

"I understand very clearly, son. I used to run a whole squad, some of which included a bunch of FNG's like yourself. I'm talking a five-minute deal here. Are you going to do it or do I have to call in some favors? Maybe talk to your supervisor, peer-to-peer. Listen. I'm not letting go of this. They used to call me the Irish Bulldog for a reason."

The young agent grinned and shook his head. "You're not going to give this up are you, Mr. Bulldog?"

"Nope."

"Okay, I'll see if I can get one of our techs to check this out."

"Good. I'll wait."

"Give me your number and you go on home. I'll call you."

Chapter 16

Almost a week later he had heard nothing. It didn't take six days to analyze fingerprints. Jack knew this. When you were comparing latents to those of a known suspect, it takes about ten seconds. You pull out a copy of prints belonging to the suspect, line them up against the newly acquired prints, then you took one of those little eyepiece things, looked at one and compared it to the other. If they were the same, they were the same and there you have it … or didn't, simple as that. When day six passed and the kid Walsh didn't call him back, there was no excuse. Jack Hannigan was pretty sure he was being screwed around.

No, they hadn't called him Irish Bulldog for nothing. They called him the Irish Bulldog because he never let go. Maybe it was time to let this kid know that he was done being polite. Maybe he needed some prompts to let him know that Jack Hannigan was not some whack job but a respected veteran of the Bureau.

He'd like to email the punk a picture of him standing next to Director Webster when he was awarded one of those Certificates of Achievement. Maybe he needed a few copies of press clippings from that trial after which a bag of crap, Squeegy Scarpone, put a contract on his life. How would that be?

It was time to give the new guy a call. Actually, he at first thought he might give the guy's supervisor a call—talk, equal to equal. But then Jack himself had never appreciated guys who tried to impress or intimidate you by going over your head. So he called Walsh directly.

"Walsh? Hannigan here."

"Who?"

"Jack Hannigan. From Philly?"

"And now from Sunny Laurel. How you doing, Mr. Hannigan?"

"I've been wondering what happened with my prints."

"Your prints? Oh yeah, the ones you thought you pulled off the old mobster. I've been meaning to call you but we got swamped."

"Swamped in Orlando? What happened? Did Goofy burglarize Harry Potter's house over at Disney World?"

"I'm not even sure I know what that means."

"Doesn't matter. Whattiya got?"

"Zero. I'm afraid."

"Zero? How can that be? Those were good latents."

"Yeah, maybe, but I'm afraid they didn't belong to Tony Fraticelli."

"Anthony Finelli."

"Him either."

"How can that be?"

"That's a question that suggests many responses."

"Who'd they belong to?"

"A woman who is not on file."

"What? A woman? There's no way fingerprints can tell you if it's a man or a woman."

"Maybe in your day. There is now a way. There have been some remarkable scientific advances since your retirement, bud. Your prints came from a woman."

"Don't call me bud, Junior."

"Sorry, pal."

"Or *pal*. Call me Mr. Hannigan or Supervisory Special Agent Hannigan. Not Harrison, not Henson. Hannigan. So, uh, maybe your tech got the prints I gave you mixed up with another set. Are you sure he got it right?"

"Positive. Anyway, nice talking to you, Mr. Hannigan. Take care of yourself."

"Wait! I know what happened. The prints I took probably belonged to the girl, I'm not sure, maybe it's his daughter, maybe even one of the housekeeping staff that had their hands all over his door after he went in."

"Whatever."

"Whatever!?! Listen to me …"

"I'm sorry, Mr. Hannigan. I've listened to you enough. My advice to you is to let this go, maybe take up shuffleboard or canasta or something."

"You little …!"

"Easy, Mr. Hannigan. We've tried to be understanding, I'm afraid, but …"

"Yeah, right, you do-nothing nobody." Jack hung up.

Chapter 17

The next day he went back to the Field Office. The secretary at the front greeted him. "Ah, Mr. Hannigan, isn't it? How are you today?"

"I'll be a lot better once I get your boys in the back moving on this."

"Then I take it you want to see Special Agent Walsh?"

"Yes. If he's not asleep."

"Please have a seat."

The wait was a little longer than during his earlier visit. Finally, an unfamiliar older man stuck his head in from the interview room. "Hey, come on in, Jack! It's great to see you!"

Hannigan rose. "Do I know you?"

"I hope so. I worked for you briefly about twenty years ago." He stuck out his hand. "Paul. Paul Dorsetti."

"Donuts Dorsetti?"

"Except down here they call me Special Agent in Charge Dorsetti."

"You're in Orlando now?"

"My final assignment."

"Surprised you lasted this long."

Dorsetti continued to ignore Jack's insults. "So. Are you enjoying retirement, Jack?"

"I'd enjoy it a heckuva a lot more if I saw some action on my request for investigation."

"I'm sorry to hear that. What's the problem?" he asked as if he hadn't already heard about it.

"You remember Anthony Finelli?"

"Yeah, sure. He was the new capo or something up there when you ran the OCR squad."

"Yeah, that's right. And now he's here."

Dorsetti chuckled. "Even the bad guys need some sunshine after a while, right?"

"He's supposed to be in prison."

"I'm sure he still is, Jack."

"He's not! He's living across the hall from me."

"Probably a guy who looks a lot like Finelli, don't you think?"

"No, I don't think. Here, take a look at this photo we got of him." He unfolded the page he'd printed on his printer and pushed it across the table at Dorsetti.

"Yeah," Dorsetti nodded. "It does look a little like him."

"A little? It's him, can't you see it?"

"Jack, to be honest, he looks like thousands of other elderly Italian guys. He looks like my father, for Chrissake. Listen, when's the last time you had a checkup?"

"Forget a checkup. I chased this wiseguy for years. This isn't a thousand other Italians. This is Finelli. Remember his mole?"

"What mole?"

"The mole on the right side of his Adams Apple. See? Okay, it didn't come out too good on these photos. Sometimes his fat covers it and my kid's a lousy photographer."

"Okay. Gee, it's great to see you after all these years, you know? I learned a lot from you. You were one of the best. I tell everybody that. The Bulldog we used to call you. Once you latched on to something you didn't let go."

"Yeah, well I'm not letting this go either."

Dorsetti reached across and put a friendly hand atop Jack's. "No, Jack."

"Whattiya mean, 'No, Jack'?"

"I mean you have to let this go."

"You think I've lost it?"

"Not at all."

"That I'm a nut case?"

"I didn't say that. I just think our minds play tricks. I know mine does."

"Maybe yours does. Mine doesn't."

"Okay. Maybe not, but I strongly recommend you let this one go. It will only cause you a lot of complications and, in the end it won't be worth the crap you'll bring upon yourself."

"What crap?"

"Uh, like you said, the guy's supposed to be in prison, right?"

"Yeah."

"So let's say you have the wrong guy and you go after him and accuse him or whatever. Don't you see the kind of potential problems that might bring upon yourself?"

"Like what?"

"Who knows? Lawsuits, acrimony, embarrassment to you and your family. You could find yourself evicted from Sunny Laurel. You don't want that, do you? Listen, I'm trying to protect an old friend."

"We were friends?"

Dorsetti rolled his eyes. "Whatever. I'm just saying you don't need the aggro."

"There won't be any aggro at all, because *it's him!*"

Dorsetti rubbed his eyes in frustration. "But he's supposed to be in prison, right?"

"Yeah, but he isn't. He's here."

"If you're right, what's that tell you?"

"He either jumped the fence or somebody messed up. I doubt that he could jump the fence."

Dorsetti nodded. "I doubt that somebody messed up. Sooo?"

Hannigan's eyes widened.

Dorsetti nodded.

"No!"

Dorsetti opened his hands. "Maybe."

"Jesus."

"Yeah. So leave it alone, okay Jack?"

As the implication sank in, Hannigan was taken aback.

"Anyway, I've got to get back to work, but hey. It was great seeing you. You know I envy you, man. Six more months before I can pull the pin. Tell me, is it really fun not having to go into work every day?"

Hannigan stared straight ahead, only beginning to grasp what had been hinted at. "Yeah," he said robotically. "Great."

"So maybe when I get out of here we can do a round of golf, have a few beers or something. How's that sound?"

"Yeah, really terrific."

"See you later, pal."

It didn't take much to make Jack Hannigan angry. Some would say that it was his default mood. But it took a lot to make him feel stunned, and right now he was stunned.

He climbed into the taxi outside the Federal Building and had a difficult time remembering his destination. Finally, the best he could do was name the facility—Sunny Laurel, but again could not remember the street name or number. The driver had to look it up on his phone.

"Does this sound right?" he showed Jack the phone screen.

"Am I supposed to be able to read that?"

"I guess we got to take a chance and see if it gets us there, huh,

Pops?"

"Don't call me Pops and don't even think about overcharging me by running me willy-nilly around town."

"You got it."

Jack sank into a deep silence on the twenty-minute ride home, contemplating Dorsetti's veiled warning. Jesus.

He was awakened by the driver. "This it?"

Jack glanced out the window. "Yeah, yeah, yeah."

He got out and began to hobble toward the entrance.

"Hey, Pops. Didn't you forget something?"

"I told you don't call me Pops."

"Whatever. You want to ride in the taxi, you got to pay the fare."

"I already paid you!"

"No, you didn't."

"I did, too." He reached in his pocket and checked his wallet. "Oh, I guess I didn't."

He handed the driver a ten. "Keep the change." Jack continued on to the front door.

The driver looked at the $10. "The fare was $16, Pops. Ah, forget it." He hit the gas and roared out of the entry circle.

Jack got as far as the lobby before he had to sit down and catch his breath. Sally came rushing out of her office. "Well, Mr. Hannigan. I never saw you go."

"What? Now we need a pass before we leave the premises?"

She laughed. "No, no. Of course not. This is your home, not an institution! I just get concerned, that's all."

"Yeah? Why?" he asked suspiciously.

"Well, we have a driver who will take you anywhere you want to go, so when some people leave on their own and we don't know where they're going sometimes I get concerned. Of course, you are one of our more youthful residents, so I should know better than to worry."

"That's right, you should know better."

"You look a little pale, though. Can I get you a glass of water?"

"Nah. Couldn't be better. Could run a marathon right now if I had to."

She laughed as if he had just said the funniest thing in the world. To herself she thought that the irascible Mr. Hannigan didn't look good. Maybe he was out of breath, maybe he had an illness coming on. Somehow she knew he was failing.

"And you know, of course, that the nurse's office is open every day until five on weekdays."

"I'll keep that in mind," he said wanting to get the hell out of there as quickly as his legs would carry him. He began to head down the hall to the elevator bank.

"Oh," she called to him. "Did I mention that tomorrow night at seven, Mrs. Tomicek is hosting a slide presentation on the trip she and her late husband took to Rome three years ago?"

"Didn't she do the same thing last week?"

"She's back by popular demand."

"Jesus."

"Oh, and, Mr. Hannigan?"

God, what now? "Yes?"

"Your apartment is located in the East Wing. The other direction." She pointed in the opposite direction from where he was walking.

"I know that. I'm just looking for the water fountain." He was thinking he should get up a petition to ship this woman to another city.

She wondered if he might not be just around the corner from becoming a candidate for the memory care ward. Under lock and key he was less likely to become a danger to himself. Maybe he was just having a brief spell? But brief spells among the elderly usually served as a forecast of longer ones.

Chapter 18

Jack wasn't having a spell. He knew this. Instead, he was in shock. Holy Christ! The Bureau *knew* Finelli was here. They've known it all along. They've just been trying to throw him off Finelli's scent. It could only mean one thing. Well, maybe two things, either one very interesting.

Part of him thought that was good. Part of him was very hurt. They had an operation going focused on Finelli but none of these dimwits had the courtesy to brief him. What the heck! In his day, even if it was a different squad—even a different agency—he would have been filled in because he was right in the middle of it, because of his proximity to the bad guy. Whoever was running the show would have requested a quiet word, during which they would have told him what they had. They'd either ask for his assistance or ask for his discretion. This was an insult!

What was a little more difficult to admit was that, absent any information, he could easily have blown their operation. Nothing was more embarrassing than that. It was as bad as approaching a fellow agent who was acting in an undercover role—maybe a guy who was part of a surveillance team or something—and walking up to the guy who's doing something clandestine and blowing his identity. It happened, usually because of the stupidity of a rookie. What you did in those situations when you spot a fellow law enforcement officer on the street was simply walk on past him. *Never ever* acknowledge him because a mistake like that could blow a costly deal, at best, or get somebody killed, at worst.

What were they up to? What did they have on Finelli and what was the game? None of his business. Now he knew that.

Damn, why hadn't it occurred to him? Maybe he *had* lost it. The Bureau was covering up Finelli's being here because they already knew. Finelli was being monitored. However he got out of prison was less important than why he remained out. They let him escape and were using him as a lure to throw the net over a wider number of conspirators. It only made sense. It meant that somewhere in this facility there were one or more agents watching him on an undercover basis. It meant that key criminal figures were in contact with Finelli here, Mob people acting as couriers while the

Bureau watched.

OR ... The only other possibility, and as he pondered it, it made much more sense: The guy had rolled. Finelli had agreed to act as an informant! He made a deal to give up his old *fratelli* so they let him out. Finelli had become a snitch! On the one hand this was a good thing, on the other it didn't make him any more likable in Jack's eyes. It only meant he had to be careful. If he exposed the fact that Finelli had become a rat, Jack could blow the whole operation. This would be a cardinal sin. You burn somebody's snitch and you blow what could be a multi-million-dollar investigation. Agents had lost their jobs for this kind of stupidity. That had to be it. This was what Dorsetti had been quietly warning him about. It couldn't be anything else.

Chapter 19

For the first time maybe in years, Jack Hannigan's mind was on fire. It was racing from one theory to another. He was alive again.

Dorsetti had all but confirmed that the guy across the hall was Finelli—the same Finelli. Okay, he didn't say yes and he didn't say no but what he said was kind of a polite backoff which was FBI code for stand clear or you might botch something we've got going. Now Jack knew it was one of two things. The old bastard had escaped or fraudulently been released and was planning a caper *or* the Bureau had let him out because he had valuable intel and they were hiding him here, which was kind of clever when you thought about it.

They definitely knew he was here. If the guy came out under illegitimate pretenses, it wouldn't be the first time a con had pulled a scam on the Bureau of Prisons. He remembered a couple of cases where mob guys bribed their case managers in the BOP to get furloughs. These were guys who should never have seen the light of day and they were coming home on holidays like college students. It happened.

Jack wouldn't be surprised if Finelli had contributed to some prison counselor's pension fund and earned himself a permanent walk. All he had to do after he got out was lay low in some place unexpected. Obviously, he couldn't go back to South Philly or he'd be picked up within twenty-four hours, assuming someone in law enforcement up there still had something on the ball, which these days there was room to doubt.

If this was the case Finelli had played it smart. He picked a spot where no one knew him and then went deep cover with a phony name as a geriatric patient in a town where there were so many old people no one paid them any attention. In fact, people averted their eyes and walked around them or in the opposite direction since no one wanted to be nearby if one of these fogies took a dive. In Florida, beyond a certain age, old people were invisible. No one paid attention. As long as they weren't permitted to drive, they posed no risk.

The guy was good, Jack had to admit. You look at him and you'd believe he had a foot and a half in the grave. He was convincing.

He looked more decrepit than Robert DeNiro in the last act of *The Irishman*. Jack would watch him closely now. Ten to one as soon as he thought no one was watching, he'd be dancing on the tables!

But wait! There was a pretty good chance that Finelli was already up to something. He was working his game right now, probably with help from the outside. Maybe it was that skirt, the pretty one who kept coming around. Maybe she was the conduit—his messenger. Jack tried to figure a way he could put a tail on her to see who she met when she left this hole. How could he do that?

Bingo! All he had to do was put Mikey on her. The kid still had legs that worked and a car that drove. Jack could have Mikey come for a visit, hangout in the parking lot then track her to wherever she went. She was probably with those South Florida *paisans*, the Trafficantes, assuming that family still ran this part of the country. Of course, he'd have to school Mikey—teach him a little technique so he didn't get burned. When it came to cop instincts the kid had two left feet.

Hold on. Jack's mind raced. The Bureau already had someone inside sitting on Finelli! That was why Dorsetti had warned him off. The last thing Jack wanted to do was burn another squad's action. That would not look good and if it happened they'd be all over him. Nothing was worse than when some klutz stepped into another group's action. That was pure amateur hour.

Still, there was no rule against him discreetly watching, taking no overt action on his own, just watching. No one would be the wiser.

The fact that the Bureau was letting Finelli play said a lot. Now Jack thought there was no way Finelli had turned rat. He was on some form of fraudulent release and, instead of just wrapping him up, charging him with escape and popping whoever the scumbag had paid off at the joint, they were letting him ride for a while. The guy must have something in the fire. He had some kind of play going and they were watching for it. They were going for the long game. Once they figured out what it was, they would tag him and everyone else involved and bada-bing, there would be *multi* Italiani taking a fall. Perfect.

All he saw was the girl who came around. If it was Jack's show and nothing else was happening, at some point he would start with her, take her out for Harboring a Fugitive, sweat her and see what she was willing to give up. Scare the hell out of her and squeeze her a little. Make her talk about what she knew about the old man's sins. But that was for later. Now he wanted to see who else was on the set, starting with the good guys.

For sure the local squad had a vantage point some place where they manned a telescope focused on Finelli's window. They probably had his room wired and manned a nearby listening post. Guys were out there somewhere sitting on him.

He got up and looked out his window. Out in the parking lot he saw a van with some silly ass sign on it indicating it belonged to a plumbing company. Yeah, right. Jack grinned. He wanted to wave, flash them the high sign. Stay with it, brothers!

He wondered if maybe he should give Dorsetti a call and offer his place as a close-in surveillance post. You couldn't do better than be right across the hall, could you? Of course, next door on either side wouldn't be bad either for listening devices through the walls. They probably had a camera in the greaseball's TV.

What Jack needed to figure out was who the Bureau had on the inside. Obviously someone working here at Sunny Laurel was not exactly who they pretended to be. Maybe it was that Cuban girl who changed the linen once a week. Or it could be that black janitor who liked to vacuum the hall ten times more than was needed? He doubted it was one of the codgers. If so, they were good actors.

Jack snapped his fingers and grinned: that Polack woman, what's her name, Sally something? She started here two months after Jack moved in, but maybe only a week before Finelli got here. There was something extremely funny about her, like she already knew who Jack was. Maybe she did! Bingo, my foot.

He raised his eyebrow and gave Merle the Squirrel a finger wave. This was going to be fun, buddy. We'll figure it out. He needed to keep a log. In the end, they'd be knocking on his door asking to see what he had. All of a sudden life in this dump was getting interesting. What he needed to do first was have a little nap. He did some of his best thinking when he was lying down.

Sally Woznecky loved her job. She was very happy here. This Hannigan gentleman was an interesting case, though. A few days ago he was almost openly hostile toward her. Unless she was seeing things, for a couple of days she felt as if he might be watching her. Yesterday afternoon when she looked up at him, she swore he even gave her a wink and a smile. Maybe he was developing a crush. Ah, well.

Chapter 20

Jack still had a good street nose. He could smell when something was up criminal activity-wise or when investigators or cops were afoot. He had spent the last two weeks watching—studying Finelli's movements and watching for his contacts, watching to see who was watching, who was talking to the gangster. He studied the parking lot, looking for surveillance teams, even looking for hidden cameras in the hallways. What he saw was absolutely nothing. If anyone was running a case on Finelli it was the loosest one he had ever seen. He had been holding back on his own probes because professional protocol required that he not interfere with any operation that his former colleagues might be running.

But things had changed in the last fifteen years. Technology had improved beyond anything he understood. It was still possible that somehow they had the guy and his surroundings completely wired and they were monitoring Finelli from afar. Maybe they had gone so high-tech that their methods defied visibility. The only possible undercover was that Woznecky woman, but that, upon further study seemed pretty far-fetched. Hannigan hated to think that he had been holding back tactically as a courtesy to another operation when in fact there was no other operation in place.

As a last ditch he decided to make contact with Donuts Dorsetti just to make sure. Dorsetti owed him the courtesy of an honest answer since back in the day Hannigan had trained him. Actually the guy had shown no obvious ability and Hannigan had carried him with the hope that the guy would come to his senses, realize that he had no talent for the business and gone into accounting or something.

Jack placed the call to the FBI Field Office. After he identified himself he waited for the call to be transferred to Dorsetti's desk. Two minutes later the operator came back on the line and said, "I'm sorry, Mr. Dorsetti is in a conference, would you like to leave a message?"

Jack Hannigan had not gotten as far as he did by accepting the brushoff. The next day, without a return phone call from Dorsetti, he tried again. He got the same response.

On the third day, he told the operator, "Let Mr. Dorsetti know I will not give up until he speaks to me."

"I'm sorry, but—"

"Just tell him. Please. If he gives me a minute, I won't bother him again."

"Hold on."

A minute later, Dorsetti came on the line, "Jack, how are you?"

Hannigan didn't miss the long-bored sigh that preceded the question. "Paul, I've only got one question. Has the Bureau got an open case on Anthony Finelli?"

"Sorry, Jack. As you know better than anyone, we can never discuss a pending investigation."

"Yeah, yeah, yeah. But you can with me. We go back and you already told me you guys were working him."

"That's not what I said."

"You sure hinted as much."

"If I did, it was unintentional."

"Paul, I knew you when you were an FNG. A very green rookie. I did you more than one solid, remember?"

"I do."

"So the least you can do is give me a straight answer and if there's something going on I promise you I'll stay out of the way. I also promise that you'll never hear from me again and that we never had this conversation. Is Finelli believed to be dirty and you're monitoring him or did he become a CI?"

"We've got nothing going either way, Jack. That's a promise."

"You're serious?"

"Absolutely perfectly serious."

"Then why the heck did you hint that you did?"

"I didn't mean to."

"You said—"

"Jack, I remember what I said and I didn't mean to lead you on. We have no current interest and to my knowledge no one else has any current interest in Anthony Finelli."

"You realize that this guy was a honcho in the Scarfo Family."

"From about 1975 until maybe 1999 or so. Yes, but nothing current. Nothing even during this century."

"They don't quit, Paul. They never change."

"But they do get old. They do get terminal, Jack. All I tried to do was for your own good. Get your mind off this stuff. We haven't even checked on this guy for maybe fifteen years. He might even be dead.

Probably is. Leave the poor old man across the hall alone. I'm sure he's a harmless nobody and you will only get yourself in trouble. It's over. Your race is won. Enjoy retirement. Do you know how I dream to be in your position with nothing to worry about? I'd love to be retired."

"Hell, you wanted to be retired the day after you got sworn in."

"Jack, I just don't want you to get yourself in trouble. That's what happens when you try to chase ghosts."

"You've got nothing going?"

"I repeat— Nothing."

"You're a bunch of morons." He hung up.

He was on his own. No one else cared. When Jack Hannigan was sworn in, when he took the oath of office to protect the Constitution of the United States, there was no time stamp on that promise. He did not say he would end the chase when he retired at the mandatory age of fifty-seven. His mission was for life. He couldn't quit any more than Anthony Finelli would quit.

Maybe Finelli wasn't a Carlo Gambino or a Joe Bonanno. Maybe a lot of people hadn't heard of the guy, but Jack knew him almost as well as he knew his own brother. He had been his primary. A good agent never backs off his target, not until the guy was dead. Or, alternatively, until the guy rolled over and became a snitch.

Anthony Finelli, he now understood, would never roll over any more than Jack Hannigan would back off.

So Jack watched and he watched and here's what he saw: nothing. There was no hint that Finelli was being watched, monitored, or covered in any way, either by the Bureau or any other agency. But Jack had one thing left in his arsenal and that was instinct. Inside of a couple of weeks with his instincts alone, he would have gotten a hint. He still had a lot of trust in his sixth sense which led him to his ultimate conclusion.

As always, Dorsetti didn't know his ass from his elbow. He had written Jack off as an Alzheimer-curdled hairball and dismissed the need for anyone in his office to inquire further. Dorsetti believed that Jack's neighbor was just some random codger, not Finelli, and to get Jack to quiet down he had implied that there was a bigger picture. Probably there was no picture at all. Finelli was not a link to a bigger crime and he had not become a CI. The Bureau of Prisons had cut Anthony loose. Who knows why? Jack had heard of cases where the BOP just let guys go because they were terminally ill—old men, rendered harmless because of the ravages of time. The prisons did this when they needed space for more lively convicted criminals. Period. Sometimes the simplest, albeit least interesting, explanation was the best one.

Chapter 21

Jack had no troops he could direct in the field this time. He had no resources: no snitches, no databases, no listening devices, no surveillance tools. This was like when he first started, before computers, wire rooms and hidden cameras. It was back to the basics. He grinned. Whatever he didn't have, he still had Jack. It was back to the basics, *mano a mano*.

The one thing he seemed to have going for him was that Finelli had no idea who he was or who he'd been, at least for now. Jack held all the cards, all he had to do was play it cool and watch closely. He would love nothing better than to hand the Orlando Field Office the case on a platter. Jack knew that Dorsetti and his bunch didn't take him seriously, but they would! "Hey do-nothings, look who I've got for you!"

He wasn't concerned that he was unaware of any new crimes Finelli had committed. Of course, it would make his hunt a lot easier if he were. There was no smoking gun, no specific crime to solve. But Anthony Finelli was a mobster, a career criminal. The very definition of being a career criminal required Finelli to continue to commit new and ongoing crimes. That the Bureau had no current interest in him meant nothing. All they cared about these days was freaking terrorists.

He just had to watch him closely. Jack's location was as perfect as it could be. What made it even sweeter was the fact that Jack was here first. If he had arrived after Finelli, the greaseball would have cause to be suspicious. He moved his easy chair closer to the door so that he could hear if someone was visiting the old mobster. He needed to be able to jump up and eyeball the visitor through the peep hole.

That his new crimes had gone undetected meant nothing. The Bureau had changed its focus. Everything now was about jihadis and white supremacists. Plus, he suspected, his former agency had dropped its standards. Jack would show them that he had kept his own. He would show them what counted and maybe they would refocus.

That there was no current smoking gun meant nothing. Finelli was middle management, just as Jack was. At this level greaseballs didn't personally go out and commit crimes. They directed them, just as Jack had directed his squad. That didn't matter or make the douchebag any less guilty. Watch him closely and Jack would figure it out. He would initiate a little one-on-one surveillance—one-on-one because there was only one of him. No big deal. If he could direct a whole squad of guys he could certainly direct himself.

The trick to surveillance was obvious. You just got as close as you could without being seen. Guys like Finelli were wise to surveillance. All the old tricks were worn out. These guys could easily spot unmarked vans on the street and telephone linemen up on the poles. They only spoke in riddles on the telephone. Whenever new people moved onto the block they were immediately suspected of being G-men.

No problem. Jack was just five feet away and he didn't look any different than the other old coots in the place. He could act just as frail and demented as the rest of them without much effort. There was no way Finelli would suspect him. He had the perfect cover. All he had to do was keep his eyes open. How tough was that?

As it happened Hannigan and Finelli had the same routine. As far as he could tell the guy never went anywhere. He was in his room. He'd come down to the dining room and now and then he might take a walk in the garden. Sometimes he used a walker. Sometimes he got pushed around in a wheelchair. The guy was only a couple of years older than Jack was. How many times had he read his DOB on FBI 302's? Finelli was eighty-one. The other thing was that the guy was making like he had vision problems. He always wore these big dark glasses like he had just come out of cataract surgery. Meant nothing. Half of these OC guys wore shades all the time because they thought it looked cool, made them look like Handsome Johnny Roselli or somebody.

Sure, it would help if he could set up a camera and hang a wire on the bad guy's phone, but he had to be realistic. Maybe he'd get Michael to drive him to Best Buy and he could pick up one of those baby cams. But then he'd have to figure out how to install and conceal it. There was no way he was going to be able to get a court order. Forget that.

He would do this the old-fashioned way. It would take longer, but so what? He had nothing but time. He grinned again. This would be fun. He would bring down the guy who had been the focus of the last chapter of his career. Make it an even once.

He pushed his easy chair over by the door so that he could hear movement across the hall. That was easier said than done. He damn near pulled out his back instead. Sitting in the chair he was three feet below the peephole. He practiced getting up to have a look. It wasn't a quick process. He settled in with a book. An hour later he heard a knock on Finelli's door and the announcement, "Housekeeping, Mr. Smith. Are you home?"

By the time he was able to lift himself to get his body over his knees, Fernanda, the housekeeper, was already in Finelli's place. He needed to work on that.

Fifteen minutes later there was a knock on his own door. "Housekeeping. Mr. Hannigan, are you in?"

"Uh, yeah. Give me a minute to get dressed." Of course he was already dressed. He just needed to move his easy chair out of the way to unblock his door. On Saturday, he would ask Michael to take him either to Walmart or Target. One of them should have barstools that were taller than his easy chair and much easier to move.

"How are you today, Mr. Hannigan?" Fernanda inquired as she always did. "Feeling good?"

"Yeah, fine."

"I will be back in ten minutes with the vacuum."

"Nah, that's okay. Let's skip it today."

"Are you sure?"

"Positive."

"Have you met your new neighbor?"

"No, not yet."

"Berry nice man. You will like him."

"Don't be too sure."

She giggled. "Yes. I think so."

When she left, he moved his easy chair back in place and settled in with his book. Before he knew it he was asleep and didn't awaken from his nap until an hour later, very annoyed with himself. He would have been relieved to know was that his target, Finelli, was also napping during this period.

He checked his watch. 1545 hours. Forty-five minutes until dinner. Tuesday. That meant there was a choice of meat loaf or hot dogs. The entrees could be generally classified as soft or extra soft. Somehow they always managed to taste the same. It didn't matter. He wasn't interested in food right now. He was interested in Finelli.

He put on the ball cap that Michael had gotten for him to shield him from the Florida son. Kept it low over his eyes, kept his head down.

Once out the door and halfway down the hall he discovered there was a fairly visible stain on the front of his short-sleeved shirt from yesterday's tomato soup. Should he go back and change? Nah. The stain would add to his cover though it might be a point of concern for that Sally Woznecky. She always seemed to be monitoring her guests' hygiene. For her they were signposts along the road to certain decline.

When he got to the dining room he headed for his table but instead of taking his usual seat he chose the one normally occupied by that jerk who called himself a show business agent. It offered a better vantage point to the seat where Finelli was assigned, two tables over. Said tablemate arrived three minutes later.

"You're in my seat," Winter protested.
"I need to sit here now."
"Why?"
"I found that one a little drafty."
"I'll probably find it that way, too."
"Nah, it's just me. You'll be fine."
"What'd you do, piss on that one?"
"No, it's fine."
"You probably pissed on it."
"Look, if you want you can have your original seat and we'll just move mine over to where you were," Jack negotiated.
"I'm gonna have a little talk with Sally about this."
"Go ahead. While you're at it, why don't you ask her for a table change? That would solve all your problems."
"Good idea."
"Yeah? Stuff it."

Ten minutes later Anthony Finelli arrived, pushing his walker. The guy looked less happy than usual even though he never looked happy at all. In fact, he looked seriously depressed, like the most depressed guy in the house, which was saying something.

Good, Jack thought. His troubles were just beginning.

For the last few days, whenever he was out of his apartment, that old feeling had come back to Anthony. It felt like he was being followed. Followed in an old folks' home? Kind of crazy, he understood that. If he had his frigging eyesight back he could figure it out but he couldn't see *ugats* more than four feet in front of him. But he felt it. Someone or something was boring a hole in him with their eyes and it was unnerving. Maybe it was a side effect of the heart meds. That was probably it.

Chapter 22

It was midnight. Jack had been up all day trying to figure a way to get into Finelli's apartment without him knowing. Back in the day, he had been pretty good at staging black bag jobs, but of course those clandestine maneuvers fell out of favor during the Nixon days. It didn't mean they were entirely canceled it just meant that a little more discretion was required. Of course, you had to be extra cagey about how the evidence discovered during an illicit entry was presented, if it were presented at all.

Back then they had guys who knew how to get past the trickiest of locks. They also had skeleton keys up the ying-yang that could get you past a surprising number of barriers. Now he had no tool to rely on but himself.

Jack knew if he could get inside he would find something, maybe a wallet with ID or some kind of clue that would prove what "William Smith" was Anthony Finelli, maybe something that would indicate what he was up to, but he wouldn't have much time, two minutes tops.

He held a pot of boiling water under the smoke detector. It seemed to take forever but finally the smoke alarm in his apartment went off. Two seconds later the alarms sounded in the hallway and in every apartment on the floor—a piercing redundant blare. It was ear splitting.

He knew what would happen next. One night staff attendant would run up and down the hall herding the ambulatory residents down to the emergency stairway. For the wheelchair bound, dedicated staff members would use their pass keys to enter each unit and help the resident into his chair and head toward the elevator. You could hear the scrambling in the hallway. If you were able to get out on your own, you were to leave the door fully ajar to show the staff that you had vacated. They would then do a cursory inside check to make sure the place was vacant.

Jack put on his bathrobe and stepped outside.

"Come on, Mr. Hannigan. We have to get moving."

"I'm moving!"

"Can you make it down the stairs on your own?"

"'Course I can."

"Good, man. Mrs. Ratloff? Don't be scared, ma'am. It's probably just a false alarm. Happens all the time."

That's for sure. It's where Jack got the idea. Once a month one of the codgers forgot to turn the heat off a burner, tripped the alarm and they all had to file down to the Great Room until it was determined to be nothing. It just never happened this late at night.

Jack made sure he was the last in line as the oldsters moved toward the fire stairs. Just before the end of the hall, he slipped into the little utility closet that housed the dumbwaiter the housekeepers used to drop the bed linen and laundry down. He cracked the door so that he could watch as the wheelchair and walker-bound rolled toward the elevator.

Finelli was second to last in that group. Finally, they pushed out Schlotzy the Farter, who tooted his way through the whole ride. As soon as they turned the corner toward the elevator bank, Jack intended to double back.

All the doors were left unlocked. He could be in Finelli's crib in two seconds. He checked his watch. He would be back out and in the fire escape before the all-clear signal sounded. Good planning and exact timing, that was the key to success in a good black bag job.

The coast was clear. It was time. He stuck his head out from the alcove.

"Mr. Hannigan?"

Oh, crap.

"Mr. Hannigan, dude?" It was Sylvester, one of the night crew.

"Don't call me, dude, please."

"Yes, sir."

"What do you want?"

"Sir, that's the broom closet and the dumb waiter."

"Of course it is. I know that."

"The emergency stairs are like five feet ahead."

"Do you think I'm stupid?"

"Oh no, sir. Sometimes we all make wrong turns."

"I was just stepping out of the way so that you could get the ones in bad shape down first."

"That's very kind of you, sir. We got them all out. Now it's your turn, unless you intend to go down with the ship."

"That's not funny, Sylvester."

"I got it from that Titanic movie. Here, I'll hold the door open for you, sir. That's it. Sooner we get down there, the sooner you can all get back to bed."

Jack shuffled aboard the elevator and let out a long sigh. Dammit! What an idiot. He doubted he could get away with pulling the smoke alarm gambit twice.

The message was slipped under his door sometime after 6 AM that morning. "If you don't mind, Sally would like to drop by after breakfast at about ten?" Of course he minded, but he knew Sally well enough by now to know that she would hound him until she had her way.

He also knew what it would be about, no matter how she would try to cloak it.

She arrived on the button as he knew she would. He had spent a lifetime with the Sallys of this world to know how they operated. Sometimes they were grammar school teachers, sometimes they were FBI secretaries, enforcing report deadlines. In his view they were ruthless so he knew he had to at least pretend that her message, when she got around to it, would be heeded.

Tap-tap-tap. He opened the door. "Good morning, Mr. Hannigan!"

"G'morning, Suzie."

"Sally. Can we chat for a minute?"

"Sure, why not?"

He opened the door to allow entry. "I must say, Mr. Hannigan, you're looking pretty good for being up all night."

"Slept like a log."

"The reason I'm here is that every month or so I like to check in with our guests just to see how they're doing. Actually, to learn how *we're* doing."

Sure you do. Right.

"You've been with us about ninety days now. How would you rate your stay so far?"

"Compared to what?"

"Well, let's say your last few months at your last home."

"There's more people."

She laughed. "Of course there are! But are you getting along with everyone? Making new friends?"

"I kind of like to keep to myself, but it's okay, I guess."

"You're comfortable here in your apartment. The food's suitable?"

"Yeah, fine."

"Is there anything you'd like us to improve. Anything you'd like to change?"

I wouldn't mind if they fired your ass, but what can I do? "No, thanks. Everything's okay."

"Well, that's wonderful. There is one thing I'd like to mention."

Here it comes.

"Yeah?"

"Your electrical appliances. What would be the first thing you would want to do when you are done with them?"

Shove them up ...? "Put them away."

"Yes. But first ...?"

"Use them."

"After that?"

Shove them ... "Um ..."

"Turn them off! Now that includes everything. Hair dryers ..."

"What am I going to do with a hair dryer?"

"Vacuum ..."

He tried not to display impatience. "The housekeeper does all the vacuuming."

"Stove top?"

"Yeah, that makes sense."

"You forgot to last night, Mr. Hannigan."

"Forgot what?"

"To turn off your stove top."

"I did?"

"Yes. You remember the smoke alarm going off?"

"It was a drill."

"No. Security was able to trace the origin of the first alarm. It was here."

"No!" It struck him that he didn't want to push this charade too far or they might want to take extreme measures. He had heard that with one old coot they had had actually removed the stove and hot plate from his apartment. The next step was to remove the coot himself from his apartment and ship him up to the memory care unit which was assisted living's version of solitary confinement.

He slapped his leg and tried to blush. "I know. I know. I figured it out when the damn buzzer started blaring. I was just kind of embarrassed to admit it. I'd made some tea then got distracted. I'm really sorry."

"You don't need to be embarrassed. We can all forget things, but my concern is that this might become, how do I say it? A pattern?

Do you think it will become a pattern, Mr. Hannigan?"

"Absolutely not! In fact, it will never happen again. Just to make sure my plan this morning is to tape a card to the lamp on the night table that says 'All power off.'' What do you think about that?"

"Why that's a wonderful idea. In fact, I might suggest that everyone here do the same. Just terrific!"

"Do you think it qualifies me to win Guest of the Week?"

"Well, it might. I will submit your name."

"That's great. Thanks."

"But I need to emphasize before I leave, that guest safety is our first concern."

"Got it."

"We don't want a fire, do we?"

"Never. Thanks for dropping by."

"Shuffle board at two."

"The fun never stops at Sunny Laurel."

Chapter 23

Jack had begun to frequent the day room downstairs and to sit on the same couch every day. It was not the most comfortable in the day room but it offered the best view of the front entrance and the parking lot. It also gave him an ample view of the oversized flat screen mounted high on the opposite wall which, at this time of day, was always tuned to *Fox News*. The channel would not change until the airing of *The Price Is Right*. Then reruns of *I Love Lucy* drew its own fan base.

The front row during the news hour was always manned by the Band of Blowhards who loved to watch as the liberals were made out to be idiotic communists. They cheered as if they stood behind the last President at the podium following every insult he delivered to the media, his former military leaders, and members of the intelligence and law enforcement communities.

Jack had never been political; it went against the very grain of being a federal agent. He had no trouble keeping his views to himself since, mostly he didn't have a position. He had served whoever was in office, since that person had been elected by the majority. No problem. If he had a position, it was that all politicians—left, right, and in the middle—should be considered suspect, usually serving themselves first. He firmly believed they were willing to compromise whatever they stood for to be embraced by whichever party they belonged. Over the years he'd had a piece or two of a few public corruption cases and few investigations gave him greater satisfaction than watching the fall of one of those hypocritical bastards. The higher the corrupt fell, the greater the pleasure. If he listened at all to the biased pronouncements that took place on the television screen, he could literally feel his blood pressure rise.

It was Tuesday afternoon which meant that Smith's girl, the one he passed off as his daughter, would be visiting. She usually made a quick stop on Tuesdays, followed by a full day's visit on Saturday. Upon seeing her, Jack reconfirmed that she couldn't be his daughter because she was slender and very pretty, whereas Smith himself was a fat ugly bastard. Genetics could not be so forgiving.

Here they came. He watched the girl push Smith in his

wheelchair through the sliding glass door and park him right out in front of the circular driveway. Where were they going? She was probably bringing the car around. Dammit! If he had kept his sedan he could run out when they pulled away and tail them.

Smith sat, his wheelchair poised at the edge of the curb. He bet that as soon as she brought the car around, he would jump up, help her put the chair in the trunk, hop in the car and drive away.

Maria pulled the car in, parked and then got out. Here we go!

Wait. She carried a packet wrapped in butcher paper and held tight with Scotch tape and put it in his lap. He couldn't hear their dialogue but it went like this:

"Be careful with this, Daddy. Please."

"Yeah, I promise."

"Seriously. It's not good for you."

"I know. You always tell me."

"Make it last. It's all you're getting for a month."

"Promise."

Jesus, Jack thought, from his position in the day room. It's a handover. I should have a camera. Why did I leave my damn phone in my room? So, the girl *was* his courier—his bagwoman. She had just passed him what was almost certainly cash. How much? Depending on the denomination, he guessed at least five grand. Did they do this every week? She visited on Tuesdays and Sundays. That would bring the greaseball about ten G's a week. Not bad. It wasn't as good as the old days but it proved Finelli was still operating.

Maria pushed the wheelchair back in the lobby and gave the old man a kiss on both cheeks. For the first time since Jack had been keeping watch the Italian looked happy as he clutched the small parcel in his lap. He wheeled himself past the day room, down the hall and to the elevator where he punched the button, the packet resting safely in his lap.

Jack too felt happy. What he just learned wasn't much, but it was another piece to the puzzle. Nope, a leopard didn't change his spots. Once a mafioso …

When he got to his room, Smith went straight to the kitchen counter, pulled out a long knife and sliced two pieces of bread from a baguette. He then cut through the tape of the packet Maria had given him and took a long whiff of a pound of the beloved prosciutto she had delivered.

Chapter 24

Later that day, just as he was once again mulling the miserable reality his life had become there was another knock on his door. Jack tucked his gun back under the cushion.

"Yes?"

A male voice. "Maintenance Department, sir."

"Yeah?"

"We're inspecting carpets, Mr. Hannigan."

"Inspecting carpets?"

"Yes, sir. May I have a look at yours?"

Jack opened the door to find a clean-cut young Hispanic man wearing the uniform shirt of the Sunny Laurel Maintenance Department.

"Hello, sir. My name is Victor. I'm with the carpet team. I just need a quick look to see if your room needs a shampoo or something. We're finding some that need to be completely replaced."

"Yeah, why not?" Jack opened the door and stepped back to permit Victor entry. He sat in his easy chair and pretended to watch *House Hunters* on the Home and Garden Television Network. Then he noticed that Victor wasn't studying the rug. He was studying Jack's mantle. More specifically he was studying the retirement plaques he had forgotten to flip over.

"Is there a problem, Victor?"

"Sir, are you a law enforcement officer?"

Somehow, Jack was tickled that the young man had not used the past tense.

He smiled. "Yes."

"Federal?"

"Yep. FBI."

"My God!" The kid stepped in front of Jack and dropped his head which was the closest Jack had ever gotten to receiving a bow. "I'm very honored."

As far as he could see, young Victor was not being sarcastic.

"You are? Why?"

"Because as long as I can remember I've wanted to meet an agent of the Federal Bureau of Investigation."

He perked up, "Is that right?"

"If I was being honest, since I was eight years old I've wanted to be one."

"An FBI agent? Really?"

"Yes. I am currently a sophomore getting my Associates Degree in Criminal Justice at the community college, but I know that won't be enough. I work here to pay for tuition. I have so many questions, but I can't impose on you."

It had been a while since Jack was treated as a hero and he had to admit that it was not something he found distasteful. His cloud began to drift away.

"Sit down, kid. I'll tell you a little about what it's like."

It came to him in the night, as did so many of his best ideas. It was a few hours after that boy's visit. The next morning, there was a tap on the door and Jack smiled. He peeked through the peephole before opening it. His caller was Victor, the maintenance technician armed with his toolbox.

"Hey, kid. How's life treating you? Come in, pull up a chair. How you doing?"

"Pretty good, sir. We've got finals next week so I been staying up late studying."

"You ready?"

"Oh, yes, sir. I'm prepared."

"That's the way. You've been thinking about what we talked about?"

"Yes, I got the addresses of most of the PDs in the state and as soon as I get through the tests next week, I'm sending out my resume since you mentioned that it might help if I get some experience as a police officer first."

"Smart. Go for the big ones. That's where you can get the broadest range of experience."

"My first choice is Miami-Dade."

"There you go. Unless you're planning on law school or a military commission, maybe accountancy, to me, that's the best angle. How's your Spanish?"

"Good. It's all my parents speak at home."

"That's a plus even though half the people in Florida probably speak it," Jack tapped his temple. "Computers. That's the future."

"Yes, sir. I think it has been for a while."

"Tricky business. Take all the courses you can. Cyber security. We didn't know anything about that in my day, but today? That's what it's all about."

"I can't tell you how much I appreciate your advice. You're having problems with your carpet or something, Mr. Hannigan?"

"My carpet? No, why?"

"Oh, I thought that's why you called my department."

"No, I just needed to get you up here. Let me ask you a question. Can you keep a secret?"

"A secret? Of course."

"When you get in with the Bureau—and I have a feeling it's not if, it's when—it's all about security, by which I mean keeping stuff confidential. Do you follow me?"

"I think so. Yes, sir."

Jack leaned closer. "Some of the biggest cases have been blown by guys shooting off their mouths."

"I believe it."

"Yes. If I tell you something in confidence, you can't say a word, you know what I'm saying?"

"Definitely."

"Not to your parents. Not to your girlfriend. Not to your best friend."

"You have my word."

Jack studied Victor's face, looked in his eyes, then nodded believing he could trust the kid. "Okay. Here's what you've got to know. I am not fully retired."

"No?"

"I went out when I reached the mandatory age, but what you need to know that as long as an agent can, let's say, provide a service, he's still in the game."

"Wow."

"Yeah."

"Okay, here goes: what do you know about the person across the hall?"

"Mrs. Ratliff? She's kind of grouchy."

"No. Not Mrs. Ratliff. Next door. Right across from me."

"Mr. Smith? He's pretty nice. He always wants to tip me when I stop by."

"I'll bet he does. Do you get along pretty well with him?"

"Yeah. I mean he always says hello when I pass him. I did a little spot cleaning a couple of weeks ago, he had some coffee stains and he said thanks. He said I made it look better, you know?"

"Perfect. Here's the deal. We want you to get in there. Make up an excuse like routine maintenance or something."

"Into Mr. Smith's place?"

"Yes. By the way, he's not the innocent old cripple you think he is."

"He's not Mr. Smith?"

"No. Maybe he is. He's just not a cripple and he sure isn't innocent."

"Wow! What do you want me to do?"

"Not much. Check his air conditioner or something, then nose around a little. Get some pictures."

"Isn't that illegal?"

"Not if you're doing it for me, kid. Not if you can keep it quiet. You'll use my phone for the pictures. Do you want to help us out?"

"For the Federal Bureau of Investigation?"

"For your country, son. For the United States of America."

"Of course!"

"We want you to look in some drawers. Get a cell phone number. See if there's any papers with a name on it. Identification. Records, like, bundles of cash.... Can you do that for us?"

"Whoo! Yes, yes. I think so."

"Without disturbing a thing, right? Leave everything in its place. Also see if you can find like brown wrapping papers."

"Brown papers?"

"Looks like butcher paper."

"Okay. And take them?"

"Take nothing. Disturb nothing, just nose around. Just take some good pictures." He handed Victor his cell phone. "You know how to work one of these?"

"Yes. Everyone does."

"Okay. Don't rush over there. In the next day or two see if you can catch this, uh, 'Smith', outside of his room, like coming out of the dining room or something or going in when no one can hear you and ask if he'd mind if you checked his room to make sure everything's still looking good. Ask if it's okay to enter his place when he's not there. If he says no problem then get in and out. Five minutes tops. Also maybe leave a rag on the carpet or on a counter so he knows you were doing some maintenance. Snap a few shots and leave everything like you found it. *Comprende?*"

"*Si*. I mean, yes, sir."

"Good man. In and out. After that don't come here directly. Just get my phone back to me, like hours later or the next day. What do you think?"

"I'm excited and honored to be of service. Do I need to be sworn in or something?"

"No. Not yet. He goes down for breakfast usually at 0845. Everything on the QT. Understood?"

"Yes, sir. Completely!"

Chapter 25

One of the ongoing debates among professionals who specialize in working with those slipping into the irrationality of dementia is the position loved ones should take when the subject becomes delusional. Is it better to play along with the delusion or is it best to attempt to correct the person by bringing him back to reality? The latter option can add to the anger and frustration that the deluded person is experiencing. Conversely, it seems nonsensical to humor or to play along with a fantasy. By following this course is the disease being fed or encouraged? Certainly it is easier than trying to fight the delusion by asserting reality.

This was the quandary in which Michael Hannigan found himself as he drove his father back to Sunny Laurel that Saturday morning after completing a toiletry run at Walgreens. He had spent two hours with his father that morning, starting with a cup of coffee at Dunkin' Donuts. It had seemed a happy visit. There was no denying that his father was feeling a little more upbeat and energetic. Michael was unable to identify a cause for his father's change in demeanor but he gratefully accepted it.

This meeting was probably the brightest visit he had enjoyed with his dad since, gosh, the day he graduated from law school, just before he had informed his father they he had no interest in parlaying his law degree into a government career at Main Justice, the FBI or the CIA. That day he had ruined the celebration when he proudly told his father that he had chosen another path in public service, namely to pursue the course of preserving human rights. The reaction he received was not dissimilar to what he might have expected had he announced that he planned on surgically pursuing a gender change. It went like this:

"The hell are you talking about!?!"

"Yeah, I'm not yet sure if I want to try to work for an NGO overseas or to fight for the cause domestically."

"Sweet Mother of Christ. What cause?"

"Dad, you may not be aware of the daily abuses that take place against the underdog not only internationally but in this country."

"Oh, Lord. You gonna move into a commune and start chanting?"

Michael chuckled. "I have no intention of moving into a

commune."

"Dye your hair purple? Get a face tattoo?"

"Not at this time. Maybe later."

This conversation occurred five years ago and Michael noted that his father had watched him closely since. He wisely decided that the subject of personal aspiration was best left unexplored until his application was accepted at the ACLU at which point his father sputtered and was unable to speak further.

Occupational conversations since then had been almost nonexistent. This morning he had fully enjoyed his father's company. The old man seemed as close to happy as he had been since before his mother had gotten sick. They had even shared a few laughs. Michael had no idea what had precipitated the change but he was elated. He had gotten a glimpse of what his Dad once had been and he would do anything if he could somehow preserve this mood.

It lasted until they got back to Sunny Laurel. They pulled into the driveway just as a red Prius was pulling out on to the street.

Jack glanced over then grabbed Michael's arm. "It's her!"

"What?"

"That car that just pulled out, it's her, dammit!"

"Who, Dad?"

"The messenger girl for that scumbag."

"Um, which scumbag?"

"Never mind. Flip the car."

"What? I'm not sure what you mean by, 'Flip the car.'"

"I mean turn around and follow her. That red subcompact, now!"

"It's gone, dad."

"It's stopped at the light. Turn around in the driveway and go after her!"

"Why?"

"I need to see where she goes, who she meets."

It was at this point that Michael realized that the ray of sunshine he had earlier glimpsed might have been an aberration. The old man had slipped back to the dark side. Michael decided that the best way to handle this was to play along. Either that or the grip his father had on his arm would cause a terminal loss of circulation.

"Okay. Let go, please." He completed the full circle in the driveway and headed back toward the street.

"Hurry! You'll lose her."

Which struck Michael as the best possible ending. But he pulled out in traffic a few cars back from the Prius.

"That's good. Hang back. Don't let her notice you."

"You want me to follow her?"

"What did I just say? Okay, the light's green, stay with her. She's turning left at the corner. Speed up."

"How can I speed up? There are three cars in front of me."

"Didn't I ever teach you how to go around obstructing vehicles without the target car knowing you're in pursuit?"

"Um, no."

"Really? I should have. Look. There's nothing coming at you from the opposite lane, swerve over and then cut back in."

"Dad, I can't do that. I don't want to get a ticket or have an accident."

Jack rolled his eyes and took a deep breath. "Maybe it's better."

"What's better?"

"That you didn't try to join the Bureau. I hate to say it, but maybe you just don't have the right instincts. Okay, now go around the corner and hit the gas. Slow down at the cross streets and maybe we'll see her again."

They sped along for three blocks but the Prius didn't reappear.

"I don't see her."

"That girl's a good driver. She lost you. I knew she was a pro."

"It may not have been intentional. There's a lot of traffic in the way."

"Yeah. She's gone. Sonofagun! Okay. Take me back."

"Home?"

"Yeah."

"We can drive around a little, maybe she'll pop up."

"Nah, take me back. I have to take a leak." Jack didn't bother to hide his disappointment and it was clear where it was directed.

"Anyway, Dad. That was kind of fun, huh?"

"This isn't about fun, Mikey. It's about work."

"So you suspect this woman of something?"

"Damn right, I do. She's the link."

"To what?"

"Not at liberty to say. Let me tell you something, you see her again, anywhere, I want you to stay with her. Don't let her see you, but follow her wherever she goes and log it. I'm sure we will see her pattern."

"I didn't see her face and I probably wouldn't recognize the car."

"Little red compact. One of those new ones. That camera on your phone?"

"Yeah?"

"I need photos. I need pictures of where she operates out of and who she meets?"

"Why?"

"I can't talk about it. Just do it. Now get me back before I urinate all over your upholstery."

Later: Michael felt like a steak. He needed a special treat. He felt like a steak and a nice bottle of cab. He selected a thick T-bone. He wasn't sure why but he always felt like celebrating after a session with his father. It wasn't that any particular visit was a victory, just that he had gotten through it. He should feel guilty. He wasn't celebrating his father's life or the joy of their visit. He was celebrating the fact that their meeting was over and, aside from a few mandatory phone calls in between, he was celebrating the fact that he wouldn't have to see the old man for another week. He was off the hook, but he needed to do some Googling. He needed to look up Alzheimer's to see if father's latest flight of fancy revealed any clues. This one was weird.

What was even weirder was that the girl standing in front of him at the grocery checkout might be the same girl his father had told him to chase an hour ago. What were the chances of that? He wasn't positive because he hadn't gotten a look at her earlier, just her car. There was definitely something familiar about her.

She was actually lovely. Long black hair and longer legs. She looked Italian. When he got through the line he hustled out the door. She had parked her grocery cart and was carrying her bags through the parking lot to—damn—a red Prius. It *was* the girl and now he remembered where he had seen her before: in the garden by the waterfall in the back of Sunny Laurel. He'd even taken her picture.

When she lifted her groceries into her car, she didn't notice that the receipt had fallen out of one of her bags and was being swept by the wind toward Michael. He scooped it up.

"Excuse me, Miss?"

She stopped and turned as he wrestled his two bags into one hand.

"I'm not sure if you want this but your receipt blew out of one of your bags."

"Oh, thanks."

"No, problem. Say, you look familiar to me. I may be wrong, but do you visit someone at Sunny Laurel, the assisted living place?"

For a half a second the mention of the place caused her to frown. "Yes, my father's there. Do you work there?"

"No, just visit. My dad's there, too."

"Oh, does he like it?"

"Hard to tell."

"Mine just moved in a few weeks ago and I don't think he's adjusting very well. He seems so unhappy."

"I hate to say it, but that might not be the fault of the place. It seems like, I don't know, like the mood that comes with old age."

"Yours, too?"

"Sometimes I think he might be adjusting better but then he does stuff that's completely crazy. It's like he can't let go of how things were when he was younger."

"I know what you mean."

"But I do believe that it gets better."

She smiled. "Promise?"

"Yeah. I promise. I'm Michael by the way."

"Maria."

"Well, I guess I'd better get going before this steak cooks itself."

"Okay, thanks for the receipt. Maybe I'll see you over there."

Chapter 26

The next day Jack responded to a quiet knock. He looked through his peephole, but no one was there. He opened the door to check the hall and Victor practically knocked him over as he slid in. He wore dark glasses and a ball cap low over his eyes.

"Victor, is that you?"

"Yes, sir. Reporting as instructed," The young man looked around furtively.

For the moment Jack didn't feel it was appropriate to point out to his young recruit that a disguise kind of defeated the purpose and that just wearing his usual on-duty uniform was the best cover.

"So, Victor, were you able to get into 'Smith's' place?"

"Yes, and I got you a shitload of pictures: every drawer, both closets, the fridge, even under the bed."

"Beautiful. Let's have a look. Sit down."

Victor was hyperventilating but he sat next to Hannigan on the small couch and handed him his phone. Jack passed it back, not really sure how to get to the Gallery. "Go ahead, make your report."

"Yes, sir. At 0859 hours on 4/22/2021, I approached SUBJECT at the elevator on the first floor as he prepared to enter the dining room. At that time he was transporting himself with the use of a walking machine."

"A walking machine?"

"Yes, a waist-high four-legged aluminum structure with two small wheels affixed to the lower end of the front posts and tennis balls stuck on the rear, for traction, I believe."

"He was on his walker."

"Yes, sir. At that time I told him 'Good Morning,' at which time he replied back, 'Good Morning'."

This was going to take a while.

"I reminded him that I was the Sunny Laurel maintenance technician, whereupon he acknowledged that he recognized me."

Jack nodded, doing his best not to look impatient.

"I told him I was going around checking air conditioning machines which had been recently serviced to make sure they were functioning properly, particularly since the hot months were quickly approaching."

"Good ruse."

"And then I asked if he minded if I used my pass key to just pop into his place to examine his machine, at which time he invited me to go for it."

"What was his attitude?"

"Like it was no big deal, sir. He just kind of nodded like he really didn't care. Like he was anxious to get to his breakfast."

"Good. Then what?"

"At approximately 0906 hours on 04/22/2021, I entered the apartment belonging to Mr. Smith, namely Apartment 211, at 5902 Belle Vista Drive known as the Sunny Laurel Senior Facility. The SUBJECT's bed was made and this investigator noted that the unit was otherwise vacant."

"No surprise. And then?"

"At that time I checked the surfaces for contents. His nightstand contained his telephone and an alarm clock."

"Okay."

"If you don't mind, I will start with the contents of his bureau and then come back to the nightstand."

"Fire away."

"In the top drawer of the bureau is where he kept his underpants. Nine pairs, white, jockey style."

Jack rolled his eyes. "Anything else in the top drawer?"

"Negative. In the next drawer down were his socks. Solid-colored, mostly black knee socks as is the fashion of his generation. Fifteen pair. A lot of socks for one man, don't you think?"

"That depends. Nothing else?"

"Just socks. Third drawer?"

"Please."

"T-shirts. The kind we in my culture call wife-beaters. Again, all white."

"Fine. The closet?"

"Jackets and a suit that he might be saving for funerals."

"Or his burial."

"Maybe. One overcoat, camel hair, which I found suspicious."

"Why suspicious?"

"Why would he need that heavy a coat in Florida?"

"Good point."

"And a zip-up jacket, blue, more like a wind breaker." Along with his narrative, he continued to show pictures of each section and each item. It was a power point presentation without the point.

"Did you check the pockets?"

"I am so sorry. I didn't think to do so."

"Not a big deal."

"He had two hats on the shelf, the kind my father would call fedora."

Jack nodded. "That figures."

"Plus, three sweaters, all of the button-up kind and seven shirts, both folded with laundry tags (four in number) and three hanging on hangers in a variety of colors. On the floor were three pair of shoes: one dressy in brown leather, one black leather and also a pair of Nikes, plain white."

"Gotcha."

"His refrigerator contained only light food staples. Milk, juice and then the butcher paper you asked me to look for."

"Now we're talking! Wait. Can you blow that up? What's that inside the brown paper?"

"It appears to be thinly sliced ham. The kind you find at a deli."

"Prosciutto?"

"Maybe."

Jack guessed that the girl sometimes brought prosciutto as a dodge. Sometimes cash.

"Oh, well. And the phone?"

"A Samsung. J-7."

"I mean did you learn anything about it."

Victor grinned proudly. "Let me show you what I found." He clicked on the next picture. It was the phone's home page which showed its number: 321-699-2443.

"Beautiful. Good work."

"Look at the next one."

"What's this?"

"Those are his outgoing calls for yesterday."

"They're all to the same number."

"Yes. Then this one."

"Which is?"

"The calls he received yesterday."

"The incoming calls?"

"Yes, sir. Two. One is from the same number he called. The other looks like it's from Philadelphia."

"Philadelphia!?!"

"Yes, sir. I looked it up. Philadelphia. That's in Pennsylvania."
"Beautiful. You did good, Victor."
"Thank you, sir. Can I ask you something?"
"Shoot."
"Is this man a terrorist?"
"No."
"Then ...?"
Jack needed to cover his tracks. "He may be nobody. He may not be the guy we're looking at. It might be someone else here. The only thing you need to know is that it's all classified, so ..."
"I must keep my mouth shut."
"Exactly. Thank you, Victor. I'll let my people know how much you helped."
"Anytime, sir. Please tell them they can call on me."
Really, what Victor provided was as good as a pen register's results for one day. A pen register was a step below a wiretap. It required a court order and it showed investigators a list of all incoming and outgoing calls. It served to show a bit about criminal contacts, associations and filled in some blanks about relationships. In this case the phone numbers and the search added up to nothing, but that's the way these things went. Sometimes they were fruitful, sometimes they weren't, you just had to keep digging.

The next morning Jack woke up, once again slightly disoriented. As soon as he got his bearings, he was overcome by the usual funk brought on by the realization that he was confined to the daily routine of an old folks' home—a death house. Then he recalled the events of the previous day—his near genius move of recruiting that maintenance kid, Victor, and the results of Victor's search. The kid was less skilled than a rookie, but hell, he meant well and look what he got.

Okay, the butcher paper was a dead end, but that wasn't too discouraging. Hannigan wouldn't be at all surprised if it was just a fake play. The old bastard probably filled up one package with prosciutto and five with cash or betting slips. Think about it. What kind of idiot at his age would still be eating greasy ham? It was a Trojan Horse. He wasn't born yesterday. Jack had seen that trick before.

The gold mine was the phone. The idiot had left his phone in plain view. It might only have two numbers on it, but that was something.

That might pay dividends.

The numbers had no value if he couldn't figure out where they were connected. In the old days he, or his guys, could figure out who they belonged to in about ten seconds, even if the numbers were unlisted, which they probably were. With the databases that the Bureau had at its command, it was the simplest of searches and from there they could figure out what else they needed to lay on a tap. Agents could then become the silent participants in all of "Smith's" conversations. But Jack didn't have access to those resources anymore. He didn't have silent participants. He didn't have anything.

If those clowns in the Orlando office gave a damn—and they did not—all he had to do was pass on the information to them and they could run with it, but they didn't care. They had written off Jack Hannigan as a senile crank, so screw them. If he called the Orlando SAC and told him what he got, the guy would probably have him arrested for conducting an unauthorized search. What a waste! The cloud over his head moved back in, with the promise of showers.

He felt marginally better after breakfast. Maybe what cheered him up was the news that Abe Winter, the alleged entertainment agent, had suffered a massive coronary the night before and he wasn't expected to make it. How would Lady Googoo manage her career? At least Winter's absence provided a better view of Finelli, three tables over.

He was able to ignore the usual breakfast conversation by focusing on his newly acquired phone numbers. Jack had not gotten as far as he had in the Bureau without some creative thinking. Some of his ideas had led to some pretty good arrests.

What he thought of was basic. When he got back to his room he dialed the most frequently called number. What sounded like a young woman answered.

"Hello?" A very pleasant young voice, no discernible urban or ethnic-specific accent.

Jack changed the pitch in his voice, trying to sound older if that were possible. "Hey, Peggy. How you doing?"

"I'm sorry. You must have the wrong number."

"C'mon, Peg. Who you trying to kid?"

The girl chuckled. "Honest, sir. Wrong number."

"This isn't the residence of Peggy Stewart?"

"No, it's not."
"Seriously?"
"Seriously. What number were you trying to reach?"
"Um, let's see. Oh, here it is 321-699-2443."
"That's this number but it belongs to me, Maria Dooley."
"Maria Dooley? Well, I'll be darned. I'm so sorry."
Maybe she felt for him because he sounded so old and she was sympathetic given the fact that she had an associate of similar vintage? "It's quite all right, sir. Maybe you just wrote it down wrong."
"I'll check. I didn't mean to disturb you."
"It's quite all right. Have a nice rest of your day." She hung up.
He looked at his phone. Did he learn anything from the call? He'd reached some bimbo with an Irish name. That was something, if she hadn't made it up. Maybe it was the alleged daughter. Maybe not. Different last name. Maybe she was lying. He needed to get his hands on a reverse phone directory.
Maybe the other number would be more revealing 445-553-3640. He knew that area code all right: Philly. He had spent the last fifteen years before his retirement dialing mostly that code. This was going to be a bingo. He felt it in his bones as he dialed.
"Law offices of Carpelli and DiMeo."
He almost jumped out of his skin. Carpelli and DiMeo! The premier mob defenders in the City of Brotherly Love.
"Yeah," he answered before he knew what words were going to pop out of his mouth. "This is Finelli."
"Hey, Mr. Finelli. How you doing?"
"Ah, you know," he said trying his best South Philly twang.
"Yeah? You feeling okay, hon? You sound like you've got a cold."
"Yeah, I guess I'm a little stuffed up."
"Hang on. Mr. Carpelli just walked in."
"Sure."
A few seconds passed then a rough voice that most wouldn't attribute to a lawyer came on the line. "Anthony? *Co me va?*"
"Ah, you know."
"I tried to get back to you yesterday."
"Yeah. Tell me. How do things look?"
"I'll be honest with you, Anthony. Not good. How you feeling?"
"Whattiya gonna do? Gotta take the good with the bad."
"Yeah? You don't sound so good. Listen, I gotta call you right back.

You at the same number?"

He couldn't give him his cell number. "Uh, yeah."

"Good. I'll get right back to you. I need to get to a pay phone."

"Sure."

Well, that wouldn't work twice. Carpelli would call Finelli's number and the best Jack could hope for was that Finelli would just think he was following up on a message left for him yesterday and there'd be no reference to the phone call made minutes before.

But Jack didn't care. He finally had full confirmation! *"Smith" was definitely freaking Anthony Finelli.* No doubt about it, Jack Hannigan had just won the lottery.

Chapter 27

So it was time to take the direct approach. Why not? Maybe he should have tried it sooner. When he heard his neighbor come out of his apartment, probably heading down to dinner, Jack opened his door, leaned his head out and shouted. "Hey, Finelli!"

The guy missed a step on his walker, turned a little, then kept going.

"Finelli, hey! You sonofabitch!"

The old man stopped and with some effort turned. "You talking to me?"

"You know who you are!"

"Whattiya want, asshole?"

Jack almost fell over. "You are Anthony Finelli?"

"So? Whattiya gonna do about it?"

"It's you. I knew it all along." The ground began to slowly spin. Jack nearly fell over.

"I'll ask you again. Whattiya you gonna do about it?"

Jack grabbed his door frame and backed into his apartment. He didn't know what to say so he closed the door to try to gather his thoughts.

Smith-Finelli called after him. "Who the fuck are you, anyway? Huh?"

No response.

"Yeah. I knew you was a chickenshit!" Bill Smith, or actually Anthony Finelli, put his right thumb to the bridge of his upper foretooth and flicked it in the ultimate Italian gesture of complete disdain. "Damn right." He turned his walker and stomped triumphantly toward the elevator.

The confrontation was loud. It was heard up and down the hall. It was heard by occupants of the adjacent rooms and it was heard by the housekeeping staff. If it got worse, the housekeeping supervisor thought she might have to report it to Sally but it would probably blow over first. These things always did.

Anthony was furious, trembling with anger. Who the hell did this guy think he was, he wondered. More to the point how had he figured out his real name? Fucking right he was Anthony Finelli and he wasn't one bit ashamed of it.

It had seemed like a good idea when he decided it was time to go into assisted living. Anthony had figured that maybe they did background checks on prospective residents and there would be nothing to be gained if they dug up some of the old news clippings on him. A phony bland name might even keep people from nosing around. Granted maybe he should have come up with something a little more imaginative. William Smith? He'd had that phony ID, for what forty years now? He couldn't even remember why he had it made in the first place. He'd stashed it in a suitcase Maria kept and had forgotten about it until he'd decided to go to Sunny Laurel.

But for what? He'd been here over a month already and they were not likely to throw him out now. Who was he hiding from? He wasn't a fugitive. He'd done his time ... sort of. Nobody gave squat about him anymore. If he went back to his true name people might start treating him with some respect. Nobody ever gave Anthony Finelli crap. He was gonna tell that Woznecky broad who he really was and have her fix his paperwork. That might be a little tricky. Maybe Maria could handle it. Maybe he'd just leave it alone. It was the least of his worries.

Fuck them. He was born Anthony Finelli and he would die Anthony Finelli. Next time he ran into that piece of shit blowhard across the hall, he'd say it again, "Yeah, I'm Finelli. Whattiya gonna do about it?"

So who was this guy anyway? Maybe the guy was from Philly and maybe he read the papers or watched the news. Maybe he knows I'm famous. In that event, Anthony smiled and felt kind of good about himself. "Maybe I still got it."

Chapter 28

Michael Hannigan rushed in the front door for a visit with his Dad. He was late. Sally Woznecky stepped out of her office to intercept him.

"Mr. Hannigan, do you have a minute?"

"Yes, of course."

"I just wanted to speak with you about your father."

"Uh-oh. Is he causing some problems?"

"Gosh, no. In fact, just in the last few days I'd say he's made a very positive turnaround."

Michael looked surprised. "You're kidding."

"Not at all. You know it's not unusual for new residents to be both depressed and a little disoriented when they first get here. To some degree, coming to assisted living means surrendering a bit of control."

Michael smiled ruefully. "Which is a little tough if you're a control freak like my dad."

"It's a little tough for anyone. No matter how we try to ease the transition, it can be both disorienting and depressing."

"That's what I've been seeing. I've been worried."

"Yes. I have to admit that I have been, too. As I said, it's not that unusual, it just doesn't generally last as long as your father's. But I think he's gotten through it."

"How so?"

"Just these last few days I've noticed a remarkable mood shift."

"You mean for the better?" he asked guardedly.

"Absolutely for the better."

"Whoa! xThat's interesting. When I saw him last I was kind of concerned."

"It's remarkable. I was wondering if you had taken him to a doctor for an anti-depressant?"

"Nope. I mean I was wondering if they might help but when I suggested it to him he said ... well, I won't tell you what he said, but he wasn't exactly in favor of them."

"It's been quite a transformation and I couldn't be more delighted."

"Uh, me either, but it could be temporary."

"Fingers crossed that it isn't."

"I'll say."

"If you find the secret, please let me know."

"I will. Thanks for the update. You made my day." He headed for the elevator.

Sally sat at her desk and shook her head. Jack Hannigan seemed to have done a 180. He was out of his apartment more and he seemed to have adopted a spring to his step. He even seemed to have developed an interest in the people around him. Old folks! They were forever surprising her. One minute they did everything possible to avoid her, the next she was their best friend. For the most part, though, they were adorable and harmless.

Chapter 29

They trudged across the parking lot from opposite directions, heads down, looking exhausted as visitors often did after a session with loved ones at an assisted living facility. Michael reached into his pocket for his keys then looked up to search for his car. That was when he spotted Maria, two cars over.

"Oh, hi! I didn't see you in the garden today," he said.

"Hey. Yeah, I couldn't coax him out of his apartment."

"How's he doing?"

"I never saw him so angry. He just sits in his chair and stares out the window."

"I think I know what you mean. That's the way my father was a couple of weeks ago."

"And now?"

"Weird. He's all cranked up. Excited, but he won't say why. He's almost manic. Is it possible that in his late seventies he's become bi-polar?"

"You got me."

"I kind of liked him better when he was depressed."

"I think I'd prefer manic," she said. "It's sad, isn't it, what happens when you get old? I wonder if it's possible to get there without being so miserable."

"If it is, I haven't seen it. All my father seems to do is try to relive his old glory days which, as I recall, were not that glorious."

"Exactly!"

"What kind of work did your father used to do?" Michael asked.

"Um, this and that. He was some kind of manager," she said, keeping it vague.

"Yeah, mine, too," Michael replied, maintaining the vagueness.

"Hey, sometime we should get a cup of coffee. I mean if you want to," she suggested.

"To be honest, after one of these visits, a drink might be more appropriate."

"A drink? That would be even better. Right now though, I have to get back to the gallery."

"You work at an art gallery? That sounds interesting."

"It can be, but I have to prepare some paperwork for an opening.

Tons of paperwork."

"Not fun, I suppose."

"More fun than a visit to Sunny Laurel. You made it better though."

"Thanks. Take care."

Chapter 30

Anthony Finelli didn't care about the squirrels outside. He couldn't see them even if he did. His eyes were too weak. Macaroni disintegration or some shit, the doctors called it. Even so, he sat in his chair staring out his picture window, though he really couldn't see much beyond the frame. There were what looked like passing shadows caused by branches waving in the wind. The light coming in actually hurt his eyes which was okay. It was better than feeling completely numb. As long as he felt a little pain he believed he was not dead.

In some ways he would welcome death. He was stuck here in this walking cemetery amidst a tribe of zombies who all seemed to be waiting for the big day. Why the hell had he stuck himself here?

At first it made sense—the whole thing. He had to rescue his daughter. To rescue his daughter he had to become something that made him worse than dog crap. He had to become a quitter—or less. A coward. He had walked out on his friends. Now he had accomplished what he had come out to do. He put the fear of God into the asshole son-in-law. That was a good thing, but then what? His goal was not to become a burden to his precious little girl and now he was here in this holding cell for barely-breathing dead people. *Temporarily,* he kept telling himself. As soon as the heat was off he was going to boogie down to Costa Rica, maybe even the DR or someplace tropical. He'd heard Thailand was nice. Some good places out there according to a few of the drug smugglers in the joint. Those guys knew how to travel.

As soon as the heat was off and he built up some strength he was out of here. He needed a clean passport, but that shouldn't be a problem. But he wondered if he would ever build up enough strength.

In reality, when he was thinking of places he would rather be, the first one that came to mind was not a place with tropical sunsets or tiki bars. The first place he wanted to be was behind the cold damp walls of United States Penitentiary, Lewisburg which, he acknowledged, was a little strange. He kind of missed the routine: the blaring klaxons every couple of hours, the stupid head counts, the crummy food. It was the company of like-minded individuals that he missed. The guys. They knew who he was, what he had done and appreciated who he had been. He missed the thousand conspiracy plans that were hatched every day up and down the tiers. He missed the ragging. He missed the respect. Those guys were alive, including the ones who were doing life. They spoke his language. Even the *melenzans* were respectfully careful around him. These people were alive and fighting to stay that way, unlike the people in this glorified dump who, even when they were young, were getting ready to be dead.

Except for this asshole across the hall. He seemed to have a little fight left in him. Who the fuck was he? Maybe they spoke a little of the same language, but he showed no respect. That guy better be careful. He pushed his luck and Anthony would have to take care of it which would not be too hard given the guy's decrepit age.

Hannigan, Jack Hannigan. There was something oddly familiar about the *gidrool*. All he knew was that the guy was a nasty old Irisher but he really didn't ring any bells. Should he? He'd give his mouthpiece Carpelli a call. Maybe he'd recognize the name.

Even though Jack Hannigan had devoted the last quarter of his career trying to take Anthony Finelli down, when Anthony was dodging the Feds, the game wasn't as personalized as it had been for Jack. Hannigan had been behind the scenes, barking orders at his squad but Anthony had never seen him and, even if he had, those Bureau guys all pretty much looked alike. They were a vanilla flavored army of robots who all seemed to go to the same barber.

Unless they were rogue supercops chasing headlines—there had been a few of them—they weren't big about calling attention to themselves or sharing their names, for obvious reasons. In Jack's case, when he was pursuing Anthony Finelli, he was always at least one person removed. He ran a squad and the squad members were the actual guys Finelli might see. Jack was more of an invisible orchestra conductor. He would direct his guys to do this or do that, frequently from the shelter of his office. Only sometimes was he actually out on the street, but never drawing the attention of the wiseguys.

Jack might believe that he had a personal relationship with Anthony. He was convinced that he was the mobster's arch nemesis. Even though Jack ate and slept with Anthony always on his mind, Anthony didn't know the difference between Jack Hannigan and

Kermit the Frigging Frog. Anthony had a better chance of ID-ing the twenty or so guys who worked for Hannigan who were always following him and planting bugs and taking pictures and conducting stupid interviews.

As far as Anthony Finelli was concerned this Hannigan guy across the hall was just some guy who might have been a mailman but now was just a cranky old bastard who didn't know nothing and who had better be careful, he knew what was good for him.

Maybe if he clipped the guy across the hall he could get back to where he wanted to be? Nah, that would be a state beef and they'd probably send him to a Florida joint like Rayburn or someplace where there might not be any fellow wiseguys, just a bunch of spics.

When he thought about it, getting back to prison might be a little *complicato*. They'd probably stick him in protective custody what with the fact that his new reputation was not going to go away. Whatever. The main problem was that he had promised his daughter he wouldn't get in trouble again and clipping a guy? By most definitions, that was getting in trouble again. At least that's the way his daughter might see it. She was a sensitive kid.

Chapter 31

Anthony wasn't hungry. He couldn't eat. Today he was in a deep funk which offered no hint that it could pass. Who was he kidding? He wasn't going anyplace. He wasn't going to Costa Rica. He wasn't getting out of here. He was dying. The worst part was that it might not happen soon. Other functions would fail. There would be further humiliation. Maybe when he got to hell it wouldn't be as bad as he imagined because he was living it here.

It took ten minutes to get out of bed his muscles hurt so bad. He could barely make it down the hall in the walker. Soon he would be in the wheelchair full-time. He could barely make it to the can. But what could he do?

At least none of his guys could see him. If they could they would turn away in embarrassment. He had come in here under a phony name. When he came up with that gambit, he thought it would fool the Feds—keep the heat off. Now he knew that the only people that were intentionally avoiding him were his own people and that the Feds didn't really give a shit anymore. They knew he was down for the count.

What did he have? Six months? One month? A week? It didn't matter. He knew it wasn't going to get any better. The pain would increase. His eyesight would get worse, if that was possible. Why prolong it?

Chapter 32

It became no secret that Jack Hannigan hated the man commonly known as Bill Smith. The staff was aware that the two men were involved in a feud. No one seemed clear as to the origin of the feud since both men seemed to be living in something of a fantasy world. It was not necessarily unusual for two residents in assisted living to develop a certain animosity toward one another and, as often as not, the root of the anger could be every bit as imagined as it was real—nothing strange there. In this case though, by geriatric standards, the war was reaching epic proportions.

At first Sally thought it would blow over. Old people's minds could be flighty, jumping from one obsession to the next with no memory of the last. Initially, Sally was worried most about the effect this little squabble would have on the other residents. Maintaining general good cheer at an assisted living facility was a delicate operation. The residents needed to be constantly reminded that there was a reason to be happy this far from their real homes and if there was any sense of strong discord, even between two people, it could upset the equilibrium of the facility. At this point she believed that neither Mr. Hannigan nor Mr. Smith was capable of actually doing harm to the other, even though they might take every opportunity too snarl.

Sally's first tactic was to initiate the 'out of sight-out of mind' gambit. She believed that if they were not in such close proximity, to wit, across the hall from each other, then they would eventually forget about it. Senior citizens were like kids. Worse than kids. They could be stubborn, cantankerous and infantile, but unlike little children they could not always be easily pacified.

This made her smile. Mr. Hannigan and Mr. Smith were really kind of cute. She recalled when studying the science of gerontology in college that seniors sometimes developed fantasy personae. These two certainly had and for some strange reason their chosen personae were at odds which each other.

They thought they were tough guys and they convincingly played that role. She knew though that in reality they were teddy bears, and as soon as she could find just the right gimmick, both would melt. In the meantime, she needed to step in and defuse the situation. Others were beginning to complain about all the yelling and the door slamming.

Obviously they needed to be separated. That was easy enough.

She tapped on Jack Hannigan's door and when he answered she noted that he looked different. Initially she couldn't decide if it was better or worse.

"Good morning, Mr. Hannigan. How is everything?"

"Pretty much as it was yesterday and the day before. Why?"

"Oh, I don't know. You look different to me. I can't figure out why."

"I'm working on something."

"That's wonderful. Have you found a new hobby?"

He gave her a mean smile and glanced across the hall. "More like an old one."

"Well, new or old, hobbies are wonderful. I wonder if I might come in for a minute."

"Why? You want to check if I made my bed?"

Sally burst out laughing. "No, no. That's up to you, I just have a proposal for you to consider."

He eyed her suspiciously but could think of no reason to deny her request.

"Yeah, sure. But can we make this quick?"

"Of course. I won't be a minute."

He opened the door wider to allow her entry.

"I don't even need to sit down," she said. "I just have a question for you."

He opened his hands, directing her to proceed. "Shoot."

"I've been wondering if you're happy?"

"That's a pretty general question. Also an annoying one."

"Let's see if I can be more specific. Do you like your apartment?"

"In relation to what? I mean I've had nicer homes. It's small, but…"

"I mean in relation to other locations at Sunny Laurel."

"When you limit it to this place, aren't they all pretty much the same?"

"Well, yes. The layouts have much in common but some have what others have considered to be better locations."

"Yeah, like what?"

"Some are closer to the elevators, a lot of people prefer that. Some are farther away and some people like that. They don't have to hear the bell every time the elevator arrives. The units on the ground floor are closer to the dining room, the lounge and the theatre, kind of in the heart of the action, if you will."

"Some action."

"There are those who don't like the fact that they look out on the parking lot and they hear a little more of the street traffic. Anyway, we just had a unit open up that is directly looking out on the garden. If you like, I can see about moving you over there. I'm giving you first choice."

"Thanks. Nope, this is fine."

"You're comfortable here?"

"Comfortable? Yeah, I suppose."

"So you don't want to move?"

He hadn't thought about it until she posed the question and the odd thing was that the first thing that struck him was that if he moved, he wouldn't be able to continue to see the one thing he enjoyed in this place: his squirrel, Merle. He knew how stupid that sounded. He would not dare repeat it to a soul. If anyone heard him say it they would think he had crossed the bridge. Christ, maybe he had.

"Why would I want to move?"

"I just thought that with your, uh, displeasure over your neighbor…"

"That slug across the hall?"

"Uh, yes."

"To hell with him!"

"You seem not to like him and we just thought it might be more comfortable, less stressful, if you were farther away from him."

"I was here first."

So like children, she thought again.

"If someone has to move it should be him."

"I will offer him the option."

"No, on second thought, keep him right here, where I can keep an eye on him."

"I will still offer him the option of moving. We like our residents to get along but we understand that sometimes there can be conflict. Real or imagined."

"You're suggesting I dreamed this up?"

"Not at all, Mr. Hannigan, I'd just love for you both to live in harmony."

In her opinion, Mr. Smith was the more infirm of the two old men and, as the more recent arrival, was most likely to be the one to acquiesce to her suggestion of a relocation. She should have started with him. She was certain she could have him out of his apartment and into another wing before the dinner bell rang. Boy, was she wrong.

He lay back on his bed and stared at her. "Thank you, Ms. Whatsnotty. I'll just stay right where I am."

"Just call me Sally, please."

"And you can call me Anthony now. Anthony Finelli."

"Pardon?"

"The name's Anthony Finelli. My daughter will straighten out the paperwork."

Good Lord. What next? "Wouldn't you at least like to see the other options?"

"Nope. I been relocated all I'm gonna be. This is it for me, as long as I'm here."

"We hope that this is the beginning of a good long stay for you."

"Yeah? I don't."

"You might want it to be if you were moved to more soothing surroundings."

"I got all the soothing I need right here."

"I understand that you might not be happy with your neighbor across the hall."

"That *gidrool?* He don't bother me."

"What's a *gidrool?*"

"Ah, you know ..."

She didn't.

"Listen, Stephanie—"

"It's Sally."

"Listen, Sally. Not for nuttin', but that guy? He thinks he might be something, but he ain't. He don't bother me, but if he's feeling unsoothed, maybe he should move, you know? Guy like that, if he's worried too much, he must be getting nervous. You never know if he gets too wound up, he could have an accident."

Sally looked alarmed. "I'm sorry, an accident?"

"You never know, guy his age. Things happen. You know what I'm saying? Did he put you up to this?"

"Oh my gosh! No, I just noticed that you two might not be getting along too well."

"Yeah? Well that *scozzo* should notice that maybe he shouldn't push his luck. You know what I'm saying? And if he got any kind of brain, he should show a little respect."

"Well, it's always nice to see you, Mr. Smith …"

"Finelli."

"Yes, and I wanted to remind you that tomorrow at ten, Frankie, our driver, will be taking a group to Target on a shopping spree! Doesn't that sound fun?"

"Uh, yeah."

"So make a list of things you need and be out front about 9:45."

"Sure. Thanks for coming by, Sooz."

Fernanda, the head of Housekeeping, reported on Thursday that she had observed Mr. Hannigan and Mr. Smith-Finelli (no one was sure of his actual name at this point) approach one another coming from opposite ends of the hallway. She wasn't sure who fired the first round, but one uttered the word, "Asshole!" And the other, "Sonofabitch." She turned and noted that simultaneously they appeared to lunge at each other—could they have both coincidentally have tripped in the same direction? Hard to say. At any rate, both missed contact and kept going. Sally wasn't sure what to make of it or what action needed to be taken.

Two days later on Friday night, one of the night people found that Mr. Smith, or was it Finelli, was facing Mr. Hannigan's door, like two inches away. Then when the staff member later passed this door he noticed a strong odor of urine in the hallway, which, in itself, wasn't all that unusual in an assisted living facility. However, on closer examination, he observed that the odor did not come from the rug but from the middle half of the door of Mr. Hannigan's unit, with dripping urine visible in the area of the doorknob. An hour later a staff member found and removed a noose, made from a clothes line hanging from Smith-Finelli's upper doorframe.

Later the same night the staff found another length of rope tied on the exterior doorknob of Mr. Smith-Finelli's unit which led directly across to inside the door of Mr. Hannigan's, securely fastening shut Mr. Smith's door. In other words, Mr. Hannigan had effectively locked Mr. Smith in his apartment.

Sally deduced that both residents had escalated their feud beyond anything previously witnessed at Sunny Laurel and that the feud had reached a dangerous level. She needed to take action. Taking action in an assisted living facility, of course, is a milder venture than taking action on the streets.

Chapter 33

During her study of the two men, Sally had noticed that even during meal times their war was in play, though they were three tables separated. Instead of Jack concentrating on his food, he instead could not take his glare off Mr. Smith, aka Finelli. If she wasn't mistaken, she had even observed Mr. Smith make what could only be described as an obscene gesture in Mr. Hannigan's direction. Well! She could at least put an end to this nonsense forthwith.

When he arrived for his dinner meal at 4:30 Jack was greeted at the dining room by Sally. She stood at the podium at the position normally occupied by a Maître d' in a decent restaurant. But this wasn't a decent restaurant, not even close, so, under normal circumstances, the podium was just a thing the guests leaned on for balance on the way to another mediocre meal.

"Ah, Mr. Hannigan. Are you having a good day?"

Was she about to try to lure him to yet another game of bingo? Did she expect an apology for his attacks on Finelli? She was either in bed with that scumbag or she didn't understand that the old *goombah* represented an ongoing threat to public safety.

"Were you waiting for me?"

"I was actually."

"What's up?"

"Well, I have what I think you will find is some good news."

"That would surprise me."

"I've found you a better table."

"Why?"

"I think you will consider the guests assigned to the new one both more congenial and more stimulating than where you were previously sitting."

"New table? Where?"

"Right over there."

She pointed to a table across from the salad bar, occupied by three codgers who looked neither more congenial nor more stimulating than the ones at his previous space. Unsurprisingly, it was at the opposite end of the dining room from his old table and did not offer the vantage point he had enjoyed to the table of Finelli. At his regular table Finelli had been seated less than five yards away from his previous seat.

"I'd like to stay where I am, if you don't mind."

"I wish you could but we've already assigned someone to your old chair."

"Move *him*. Not me."

"Um, because of that gentleman's specific health problems, which I'm not at liberty to discuss, it is more appropriate that he remain closer to the restroom. Now come on, give this a chance. I think I've joined you with a trio of like-minded individuals who are sure to make your stay here a lot more enjoyable."

He didn't today have the energy to mount a counter argument.

She led him to his new table and made the introductions to his three new tablemates. As it turned out these old men weren't as close to death as they appeared from a distance. They were very much alive, at least to the point that they never shut up. They were stimulating all right and what they stimulated was indigestion. He knew he would learn to hate each of them.

"Fellows, let me introduce you to your new table partner. I hope I'm not speaking out of turn when I tell you that he too served this country. Mr. Jack Hannigan. Our most senior resident here is Morris Trueway, formerly of Indianapolis before his retirement to Florida."

Morris, as everyone was forced to immediately notice was an ardent supporter of the last President. To make that clear, he wore a bright red hat which proclaimed that he intended to Make America Great Again.

"You may have already met Mr. Stephen LesCroates since he is our in-house chairman of the Veterans of Foreign Wars." If there was any doubt about this Mr. LesCroates wore a black baseball cap emblazoned in gold with a picture of a destroyer and the years which declared he had served in the Navy during the Viet Nam Era.

"And of course, Chuck Naismith, who you might be interested to know is building a Sunny Laurel chapter of the National Rifle Association."

"Get behind me, pal," declared Chuck. "And we'll get that rifle range where we can keep sharp our AR-15 skills."

"There, see?" Sally joyfully declared. "You are now with like-minded individuals! Enjoy your meal gentlemen."

"What's she talking about?" LesCroates inquired.

"Whattiya mean?" Jack asked.

"About you being like-minded?"

"I guess it's because I'm a retired civil servant."

"Yeah? What outfit?"

Jack studied his new dinner partners. He immediately knew that if he told them the truth he would have to listen to their stupid opinions. "Um, the Social Security Administration."

The other three looked at each other trying to come up with something they hated about the Social Security Administration. None was able to immediately pinpoint an issue, so they snorted and looked at their table settings.

He wouldn't have been shocked if they all stood and goose-stepped over to the salad bar. But they did not. He was not at all surprised to learn that his three new fellow diners were much more interested in telling him about themselves than learning about him. Their goal was to declare their patriotic credentials to be superior to anyone in the house. They were not, at least initially, even vaguely curious to know more about him. He sighed deeply as it became clear that Sally Woznecky had placed him firmly in the middle of the local chapter of the Band of Blowhards. He might enjoy, at least for a moment, exposing the shallowness of their heroic backgrounds. Could this woman Woznecky actually believe that Jack Hannigan was one of these idiots? Worse, was it possible that he was one?

In another time, he might have been these would-be heroes' hero. But then he had blinked and now, were he to be honest about his own background, each would have found both the grounds and courage to question him. At best he could expect that he would be required to hear from each of them their theories about what was wrong with the criminal justice system. As if he cared.

He knew just by looking that Chuck Naismith had probably built a massive armory in his home, but the skinny little twit had probably never aimed one of his guns at a live person. More to the point, he had never had a gun pointed at him. Guns for Chuck were sex toys, extensions of what was bound to be a microscopic organ.

While LesCroates might well have served aboard the USS Whatever during the Viet Nam Conflict, in all likelihood his role was not much more dramatic than being an oiler on a ship that was anchored well out of range of the most aggressive NVA Mig.

The nearly fluorescent Morris Trueway, in his stupid Hawaiian shirt, was like many right-wing true believers. Jack was sure that Trueway's sense of disenfranchisement from the government was caused by his belief that all non-Fox news was fake and that former law enforcement or intelligence officers were members of a Dark State. With the last President, things were being corrected and the swamp was being cleared. We were almost free of all the colored, the Mexicans, the faggots and the general populations of shithole countries. Then the election was stolen and we're back to where we started.

Bunch of losers, Jack confirmed. He craned his neck, but no matter the angle, he no longer had a view of the chair where Anthony Finelli took his meals.

"You were with Social Security, Hannigan?"

"Yeah, in Philadelphia."

"Sounds boring."

"Oh, it was."

"You guys managed to be so boring that we never got what was our due."

"I'm sorry."

"You want to sit at the men's table. You got to be tough."

"I'll try."

"In 'Nam we had a name for guys like you. Candy-ass. No offense."

"None taken."

"You're not a fruit are you?"

"Absolutely not."

"Didn't think so. I can spot 'em a mile away."

"Stick with us, Jack. We'll help you grow a set of balls. Help you figure out the truth and we might even let you join the fight."

"Gosh. Thanks."

As he had intended, this brief assault pretty much ended inquiries into Jack's history. These days for Jack it would have been easier to wake up in a city where no one spoke English. It might even be easier to be locked alone in a cave.

Moving Jack across the dining room did nothing to de-escalate the conflict between him and his nemesis. Over the next several days the battle intensified.

Chapter 34

Michael came down the stairs after a visit with Jack and ran into Maria just as she was also leaving the elevator.

"There you are. It's Maria isn't it?"

"Yes, it is and I'm afraid I never got your name."

"I'm sorry. It's Michael. Michael Hannigan."

"Ah, and how was your father today?"

"Angry. Angry and cranked up."

"You know mine was the same. I can't get over it."

"Beats depression, right?"

She pondered that. "Good question. I haven't decided."

"Anyway, I was hoping maybe today we could have that drink."

"Great idea. Two would be even better."

"There's a cocktail lounge I saw just a couple of blocks from here. We could go in my car and I can drop you back."

"Perfect."

As they were heading out of the lobby, Sally Woznecky stepped out of her office. She had spent the previous night considering the all-important question of liability which governed almost every decision in this assisted living facility. She had decided that her actions to date might be deemed ineffective and she needed to try to dismantle the Hannigan-Smith feud from another angle. It was time to shift the issue of liability to other parties.

"Excuse me, Mr. Hannigan. I was wondering if I might have a word."

"Uh, yeah sure," he glanced at Maria.

"I'll wait by the waterfall."

"Actually, I was hoping to speak with you both."

"Uh-oh. Sounds like rates are going up again."

"No. Not at all. Please. Come in and sit down."

They sat at her desk wondering what was up.

Sally took a breath. "It's your fathers."

"Both of them?"

"Yes, unfortunately. Both of them."

"What have they done?"

"They do not get along. Actually, they seem to hate each other. Apparently with a vengeance."

"My father seems to hate everything right now, but that's not uncommon, is it?" Maria asked. "I mean for people of that age."

"I'm not sure what else they hate but they certainly hate each other and I'm worried about how this will end."

"Actually," Michael said. "In some ways, though he's angry, my father has never seemed happier than when I've seen him in the last couple of weeks. I mean since he's retired. You've said yourself that you thought his mood has gotten better."

"Be that as it may, the two are having a feud, and it's escalating."

"What are they doing?" Maria asked.

Sally pulled out a steno pad where she checked her notes. "Two weeks ago Sunday, urine was splashed on Mr. Hannigan's door. When we inquired about it, Mr. Hannigan denied responsibility."

Michael's eyes widened. "He said he didn't urinate on his own door? He was probably embarrassed. My father's bladder control might not be what it once was. He was probably trying to get to his toilet without success."

"How does that involve my father?" Maria inquired.

"Mr. Hannigan insisted that your father was responsible."

Michael turned to her. "I'm sorry, Maria. As I said, my father was probably too embarrassed to accept blame."

"Well, that's possible, isn't it?" Maria turned to Sally indicating it sounded plausible.

Sally continued, "There was indeed urine, according to Housekeeping, splashed on his door and the stream, according to Housekeeping, started at the doorknob."

"Who knows?" Michael conceded. "Maybe my dad was fumbling with the lock trying to get in and …"

Sally shook her head.

"You still believe my father was involved?"

"Yes."

"Why?"

"On the night in question one of our workers saw Mr. Smith standing less than two inches from Mr. Hannigan's door, facing it, and when the worker approached, Mr. Smith moved away and appeared to be adjusting his trousers."

This time Maria's eyes widened. "Uh-oh."

"Yes. So we asked Mr. Smith about it."

"And what did he say?"

"He gave a rather nasty smile and suggested that next it would be feces. Those, by the way, were not his exact words."

"My God! My father said that?"

"He said that."

"I'm so sorry, Michael. I will speak to him."

Sally held up her hand. "It did not end there. Three days later our security officer found a noose taped to the frame of Mr. Smith's door."

"Ah, geez. My Dad?"

"That's our guess. We don't know where he got the rope."

"I do," Michael said, looking at his lap. "I'd got him a twenty-foot length at Walmart because he said he needed it to hang up his wet socks."

"We have driers, Mr. Hannigan. The noose apparently only used five feet of rope. At any rate, following another incident, precipitated by one for which we suspect your father was responsible for initiating, Mrs. Dooley, Mr. Hannigan found a use for the remaining fifteen-foot length."

"Oh, no. What did my father do first?" Maria asked.

"It appears that he jammed a piece of used chewing gum into the lock on Mr. Hannigan's door. We had to replace the whole unit. Which was followed by …"

Michael braced himself.

"When Mr. Smith was in his apartment sleeping, we believe Mr. Hannigan tied a rope around Mr. Smith's exterior door knob, pulled it tight and fastened it on the interior doorknob of his residence, effectively locking Mr. Smith in his apartment. I don't have to tell you the consequences if there had been a fire."

"No," Maria said gravely.

"We used to do that in the college dorms," Michael said shaking his head with some amusement.

"Do either of you have any insight as to the source of this animosity?"

"No."

"No."

"And neither of them appears willing to enlighten us. This has got to end now," Sally insisted.

"I agree," Maria said.

"Unbelievable!" Michael exclaimed.

"Please believe it. We have seen some unusual behavior from our seniors, but this, unfortunately, takes the cake. It has to end."

"Yes," Maria agreed.

"We can't permit this to escalate further. Obviously, I've spoken to the two of them separately and neither is willing to admit his behavior, nor does either express remorse. I have also offered to separate their apartments. I currently have a vacant unit over in Tropicana, the wing on the far side, but both insist that they will not be moved. They want to stay exactly where they are."

"My father can be pretty stubborn," Michael nodded.

"Tell me about stubborn," Maria chimed in.

"Which is why I'm speaking to you now. I'm afraid that if there is another episode, out of liability concerns, the responsible party or parties will be evicted. I hope that you both will talk to your fathers immediately and advise them of the potential consequences."

"My God. Where will I put him next?" Maria asked.

"Please speak to them right away."

He tapped on the door and was surprised when his father jerked it open almost immediately.

"I thought you left," Jack said as he stuck his head out and stared at the door opposite, then gave a furtive look up and down the hall.

"Yeah, I tried, but Mrs. Woznecky grabbed me before I got to the parking lot."

"She's a prying old biddy, isn't she?"

"Actually, she's probably at least 30 years younger than you and she seems pretty nice. Just concerned."

"Why? Is it because I don't show up for Bingo?"

"I hope she's mistaken but she seems to think you've declared war on your neighbor across the hall."

"She's mistaken and it's none of her business."

"She believes that the two of you are engaged in increasingly dangerous behavior to sabotage each other."

"Dangerous for him maybe. Not for me and she'd better stay out of it if she knows what's good for her."

"Do you mean that it's true?"

"How should I know? I don't know what she told you."

"She said she's asked the two of you politely to cease and desist from destructive behavior."

"I wonder how she'd feel if she got charged with Interfering With a Federal Officer. How would she like that?"

"Dad, what in the world are you talking about? Are you engaged in some sort of vendetta against the poor old man across the hall?"

"Do you know who that 'poor old man across the hall' happens to be?"

"Uh, no."

"Anthony Finelli, that's who."

"Who's that?"

"He was a crew chief in the South Philly mob, the Scarfos, to whom I devoted a good portion of my career trying to arrest."

Michael looked skeptical. "C'mon Dad, really?"

"I may be old, kid. But I'm not crazy. My squad tracked that bastard for years. I don't forget a face."

"I'm not so sure that's true anymore."

"It's true, dammit!"

"Okay, okay. Calm down. Even if it is Finucci ..."

"Finelli! Anthony Finelli."

"Even if it is Mr. Finelli. He's an old man now."

"That makes us even."

"Yeah, but that gentleman looks like he's blind and he can't walk anymore."

"That's bull. He's faking it. He's like that Capo in New York who used to walk around Greenwich Village in a bathrobe, what's his name?— Vincent "The Chin" Gigante, trying to convince the court that he was crazy but he was crazy like a fox. Believe me, Mikey, this *goombah* across the hall is fine and he's up to something. I feel it in my bones."

"Dad, does that justify trying to lock the guy in his apartment? Trying to cause him to have an accident? What if there's a fire or he gets seriously hurt? You could be charged with a felony. You could get sued. Hell, maybe even I could get sued. You're putting yourself and my job in jeopardy."

"I'd sue him back."

"Dad, please ..."

"And that bimbo who comes to see him. Trust me. She's his runner. She's carrying messages, probably contraband."

"That bimbo happens to be his daughter. She's completely respectable and I can tell you for a fact, she happens to be a very nice girl."

"Yeah? My foot! Did you get a look at him? She's too pretty to be the daughter of a fat ugly sonofabitch like him."

"Dad, whoever the man is, you're breaking the law by trying to cause him discomfort and very probably a serious accident."

"You think he's innocent? Do you know what that crazy old bastard has done to me?"

"Then report him when he does it. Mrs. Woznecky will take action. She's about to anyway. You're going to get thrown out of here, the both of you, but I can tell you right now, that if he chooses to take action against you with all of his obvious disabilities, he would win. Back off before you get into serious trouble. This is not how a decorated agent of the FBI acts. You took an oath."

Jack dropped down in his easy chair. For the moment he was beaten. Michael was right. He had taken an oath. He had promised to defend the Constitution of the United States against all enemies. He had promised to do that *lawfully*. If he got caught pulling some prank against that dirtbag across the hall, then yeah, maybe he could get in trouble. The last thing he ever wanted to do was embarrass the badge.

"He's up to something, Mikey."

"Maybe so, but if he is, he has to be caught lawfully."

Jack closed his eyes, very tired all of a sudden. "You're right."

"Promise me, Dad. No further shenanigans. You're putting us both at risk."

"I think I'll take a nap now."

"Promise me."

"I promise."

Maria tapped on her father's door. It took Anthony a while to get out of his chair to answer it. "Maria, my love. You came back. Did you forget something?"

She's angry. "Daddy, you promised."

"What'd I promise?"

"No more trouble. You promised you were finished."

"What are you talking about?"

"You know what I'm talking about. That man across the hall."

"He's a *gidrool*. I can take him."

"You are in no shape to take anyone."

"I can take *him*. I don't care what he used to be."

"What do you mean 'what he used to be?'"

"I heard on the street, the guy is FBI."

"Heard on the street?"

"My lawyer. He told me the jerk-off ran the squad that used to dog us."

"Oh, please, Daddy. That can't be."

"It's true!"

"Well, if it's true," Maria said, not believing a word, "then you have to be careful. I'm sure he's got plenty of friends."

"I got friends, too."

"Not anymore. You came down here and you promised me it was over. You retired. Did you lie to me?"

She sat on his couch and began to cry softly.

"I didn't start this," he said.

"Did you lie to me?"

"I didn't lie."

"I want you to move to another wing. Sally said they have a vacancy on the other side of this building."

"I'm not moving because of that jerk!"

"Daddy ..."

"Okay. No more *agita*. But I'm not moving. I'll just ignore him."

"Promise?"

"Yes."

"Otherwise, you'll be evicted. Then you have to come home with me."

"I'm not coming home with you. I'm not going to ruin your life."

"It wouldn't ruin my life."

"Having a crippled old man in your house? It would. How you gonna meet a nice young man?"

"Actually, I might have. Unfortunately, you might not think so."

"Not another jackass, please."

She smiled through her tears, "No, not this one, but you wouldn't like him."

"Why?"

"It's too early to tell you. Anyway, I want you to leave Mr. Hannigan alone."

Chapter 35

They sat across from each other in a booth. Michael with a glass of Scotch, Maria with a glass of Chardonnay. After each took healthy slugs from their glasses both looked at each other and burst out laughing.

"What are the chances that these two old men would go at each other like this?"

"Unbelievable," Michael repeated.

"And hilarious if it weren't true."

"According to my Dad, it isn't, but he had a glint in his eye which tells me he was lying."

"Well, it kind of explains one mystery," she said.

"What's that?"

"Last week my father asked me to pick up a can of motor oil that he could keep in his room."

"Did he say why?"

She nodded. "He said it was needed just in case I turned up here a quart low."

"My God! He was planning on torching my father's apartment."

"No, I don't think so. Then he would have asked me to bring a gas can."

"What in the world was he going to do with it?"

"Who knows how he thinks? Maybe pour it on the floor to make your dad slip?"

"Jesus! Is it dementia?"

She opened her hands.

Michael shook his head. "My Dad is convinced your father is an Italian gangster."

"Mine thinks your Dad is a rogue federal agent."

They both laughed nervously then looked away.

Michael shrugged. "The weird thing is, it's been years since I've seen him so … I don't know, happy isn't the word for it. More like triumphant. Justified. Like he has a cause again which he's determined to fight for … and win. It's funny. But his mood changed when I told him it had to stop now or he'd be out on the street and that I would refuse to help him find a new place."

"Mine looked like he was ready to cry when I told him I wouldn't

visit him again," she said.
"They are children."
"About to be expelled from assisted living."
"What do you say? Another round?"

Within five minutes of Michael's departure, Jack felt the dark cloud sweeping toward him until it parked squarely over his head. His heart felt as if it had been dropped down a mine shaft. He was as depressed as he had been the day before he recognized Finelli as his new neighbor. Out of the corner of his eye he detected movement from his window. It was the squirrel balancing on a branch staring in at him.

How had he ever been distracted by this obnoxious rodent, this scavenger? If he had a gun right now he'd shoot the sonofabitch. Actually, he had a gun ...

Chapter 36

Problems. That's all that Anthony had left. Fucking problems. At eighty-one, sixty as a successful made guy—all added together—in the end it meant nothing. *Niente!* Everything he'd stood for, had fought for and had defied the Feds for, was worthless. The Government had accomplished its goal. Eighteen years into his sentence—just a little more than half done—and he had been written off, actually written out. All because of that ugly sugar disease, diabetes.

So what did the Bureau of Prisons pull? This is what they pulled: to cut down on funeral expenses, maybe law suits, guess who they let out first: him, because he had served a significant portion of his sentence and was now considered harmless. Harmless! Let me tell you, the biggest insult you can give to a wiseguy is to call him harmless. You might as well accuse him of being a fruit. Somebody in Washington, at the Department of Justice or somewhere had made the decision that Anthony Finelli, because of his age and his health was unlikely to commit another crime.

They offered him a release contingent upon him having a place to go just as long as it wasn't back to his base of operation, which, of course, was South Philly. They called it a compassionate release. Compassionate my ass.

He didn't have to go. He could tell them what he always told the cops: "Go fuck yourselves." He might only have a few years left to breathe but his honor required that he stay where he was—with his crew. Prison wasn't that bad and he had a responsibility to his people.

But the truth was that Maria was having problems. Her problems were with her husband, that irritating little Irish *scazzook*, Jim Dooley. Initially, it was with some relief to Anthony that the man Maria chose to marry was not in The Life. He wasn't even Italian. He was from an unblemished family which had apparently followed the path of the straight and narrow. His daughter was not marrying into the Mob. Dooley was a legit financial manager. What could go wrong? But it turned out he liked to push Maria around when the stock market went down. Young Mr. Dooley didn't have the balls to stand up when he took a loss, so he took it out on Anthony's daughter. He pushed her around, even slapped her around! It didn't require a great deal of imagination to figure out what was going on when, on visiting day, his daughter showed up wearing dark glasses.

Jim Dooley knew a little bit about Maria's old man, but while he once might have been in awe, now he didn't give a crap. Anthony was in the can and all of Anthony's backup was similarly situated. That or they had too many problems of their own to respond to Anthony's request for a little marital counseling on Maria's behalf.

The only thing Anthony thought of when he was offered a release was that it was an opportunity to permanently straighten out that little *pezzo di merde*, Dooley. He'd give him something to manage. Manage this, you mick garbanzo. But what happened when Dooley heard he was coming? Guess who hit the wind. He knew what was next, the punk. When he finally moved into Maria's home in Orlando, Anthony looked like death warmed over. Dooley might not have been so scared if they actually met in person, but he was gone.

So then Anthony was out with nothing to do. Nobody to intimidate, just his daughter to drive nuts. A mostly empty house to do nothing but faint in. First thing he did once he'd taken care of the Dooley problem was see what he had to do to get back in the joint. He contacted everyone he could think of starting with the warden but nobody returned his calls. He let the guys know he was coming back by hook or crook but, if he were honest with himself, none of them seemed to really give a shit. That was the tough part. He couldn't even think about it. He could almost live with being written off by a frigging prison, but by his own crew? His boys? That hurt.

If he were to be *really* honest? It don't pay no dividends growing old. When he drifted off, he would sometimes dream about taking a stroll down Passyunk Street in South Philly, but really? These days he probably couldn't make it a block.

Like most mobsters, Anthony Finelli took a fast buck wherever he could find one.

Finelli's tentpole racket was gambling and related enterprises. He had run a long string of bookmakers and was behind most of the illegal poker machines in the city. In addition, the other major games and illegal casinos paid dues to him. His auto parts business was just a front for everything else. He also got a cut from the usual non-affiliated crooked enterprises in his neighborhood. He was not known for extreme violence but his people didn't tolerate unpaid debts, hence all those costly little extortion counts in the superseding indictments. Whattiya gonna do, close your eyes to the deadbeat losers? His guys were earners and they made Anthony an earner who kicked upstairs a due percentage of his earnings as required. At first blush it looked as if Anthony was pulling down a fortune, but he had his overhead, a good portion of which went to an unofficial fund of the City's police.

Finelli had taken his fall after five years of investigation. He went down the usual way, but sadly—actually humiliatingly—as far as Jack Hannigan was concerned, the mobster's fall was not orchestrated by the FBI. It was the goddamned IRS with their adding machines and calculators that got their hooks in first. It was simple math! All they did was add up the mobster's assets and subtract what he declared. The IRS piggybacked off Jack's squad for some sexy filler. A number of guys who owed Finelli and could not pay agreed to wear a wire. Two of Finelli's own people decided they'd more enjoy Witness Protection than remain mute and, bada-bing, down he went for thirty-five.

Most people would think that the worst time in Anthony's life was when he was sentenced to prison. Actually, going to the joint turned out to be much easier than some might expect. He had been sixty-three and a widower when he was sentenced. It would have been different if he was a black or a spic or a skinny unaffiliated white. Any of those and he would have been faced with some very real daily challenges. It would be dangerous. But, as an older guy who came in from a mid-level position in the most feared criminal organization in the world, he was part of a protected species.

There was a lot to be said for entering the can as a senior citizen. The daily routine wasn't overpoweringly boring. His age put him past the point where he needed constant stimulation. Sure, you might miss a glass of wine and an extravagant meal, but you could occasionally put together a good feast by combining the care packages from home with fellow members. You could exercise moderately, go for walks and even watch cable TV. When it suited you, you could enjoy a game of checkers. Nobody would cause no *agita*. If he were honest his last decade at home hadn't been all that pleasant because the Feds were constantly on his back and the rat ratio in the ranks was climbing. Honestly, aside from his declining health and worrying about his inability to protect his daughter from that conniving cucumber, prison wasn't a bad life.

Then he got to Sunny Laurel and the skies got dark. Depression? "The fuck is this?" he asked himself. "This don't happen to me," he sighed. Worse, there was no cure—at least not in this facility. When he tried to find ways to cheer himself up, he found nothing.

Ah, well, even with the asset seizures that the Government had initiated, they hadn't found it all, so money wasn't a problem. He figured that he could lay low at Sunny Laurel until his little girl was able to pull it together and maybe find a new young man. When that happened he could hit the road. Maybe Costa Rica, maybe … then he thought about it realistically and the rain came down. In torrents.

Chapter 37

There are almost as many retired Italian mobsters living in Florida as there are Cubans. They emigrate from the Northeast and Midwest like swallows to Capistrano except, once here, unlike the swallows these guys stay. They represent all five families, even those which may be in conflict with each other. Mostly, once they reached the arthritic stage, they were at peace with each other. Each sub-family had an appointed ambassador whose job was to interact diplomatically with representatives of other families and also to welcome newly emigrated members of their own clan. If a member was able to relocate to Florida upon release from an institution it was custom that the releasee be welcomed by his respective emissary and be gifted with a thick envelope designed to ease his resettlement. It was kind of like the Welcome Wagon without the fruit.

When Anthony Finelli came to Orlando there appeared, at least to him, to have been an administrative glitch. None of the boys made a donation and there was no envelope. There was no greeting whatsoever. Initially, Anthony understood this. His release was kind of sudden so perhaps the word had not gotten out. Maybe there were other issues. With the Mob there were always other issues that might distract or disrupt ordinary custom, so Finelli didn't get too upset. After a few weeks though he needed to correct this oversight. While he did not need the contents of the envelope, he needed the respect. So he initiated the reach-out saying, in effect, "Hey, what the fuck?" Shortly after that he got a call from the guy who was the current rep from South Philly and it seemed that the oversight was on its way to correction. But no.

It was Tuesday, wasn't it? So Monday was yesterday. Monday was the day that Frankie "Little Sausage" Gravanato had said he'd drop by with his greeting. Little Sausage was the only wiseguy he had contacted since his release. The kid was his designated link with the Mafia diaspora and he was the one that was the assigned greeter for his family. Little Sausage was living in Palm Beach now but was still very closely wired to South Philly. He had relocated down here as did dozens of others from the Tri-State area a few years back and was now South Philly's local rep. That they had left the City of Brotherly Love did not mean they had relinquished all of the action, it just meant that they had built in a layer of administration to keep an eye on things so that they could more subtly make their withdrawals. You might say they were operating remotely, socially distancing themselves from the Feds. The overall operation continued to run pretty well if you factored in the number of guys who were on federal hiatus.

Still, in Anthony's case, they seemed to have dropped the ball when it came to observing certain traditional obligations. Anthony used to like Little Sausage. He thought the kid might have a reasonable future and had even supported his minor rise through the organization, but he had noted in his most recent telephone contact that the guy seemed somewhat less focused, less genuinely concerned about the state of Anthony's well-being. In short, he'd been acting like he had better things to do than welcome Anthony back into the fold and apprise him of the current state of their union.

Of course, Little Sausage was just one man, a cog, but his simple affront was magnified because Anthony was having a difficult time ignoring his own aches and pains. You know how it is when you have a couple of little things wrong with no bright spots? It had become harder and harder to get up the energy to push himself out of bed. Once he was upright, it was only with God's help that he could grab his walker and shift his weight over it enough to stand. Then what? He had tried to ignore it but the truth was that his eyes were getting worse. Macaroni disintegration. You wanted macaroni disintegration you needed to try the noodles at Sunny Laurel!

If he were honest, it wasn't the envelope he cared about. It was the insult that came from the lack of that personal touch. Little Sausage was the last remaining link, his only tether to the old days when he could walk down the block and sit at the club and hear the news.

If Anthony were honest, Little Sausage was a punk. Back in the day Anthony barely paid attention to the kid who probably wouldn't have gotten in if it wasn't for his old man, Sal "Big Sausage" Gravanato. Big Sausage had a sense of responsibility. He never would have skipped an appointment. He never would have left Anthony sitting here unvisited. In fact, when Big Sausage had himself been physically going downhill, Anthony always made sure the old man knew they still cared. He visited the guy a couple of times a week after Big Sausage was so fucked from the stroke he couldn't talk no more. He'd sit by the guy's bed and hold his hand and reminisce about the old days. Now and then Big Sausage would manage a responsive squeeze but that was the best he could do. Anthony had shown Big Sausage respect! You didn't forget respect even if the guy on the other end couldn't do no better than crap in his pants. You know what I'm saying?

He could just cry when he thought about it, though he wouldn't shed a tear in front of these weakling *gidrools* who surrounded him now. They might misinterpret it and consider him a fellow fag or something.

He threw down his fork, got up with some effort and pushed the walker out to the day room. He sat at the end of a couch that faced the big flat screen TV which was always on *Fox News* because that seemed to be the one channel all of the people here agreed on, though it was hard to tell. Most of them stared blankly at the screen, like this old broad without the teeth at the other end of the couch.

The day room was where the residents were supposed to interrelate, socialize and share their opinions about the events of the day. Anthony didn't plop down here to socialize. He plopped down here to rest because he was too tired to make it all the way to the elevator. He'd sit a couple of minutes before he pushed himself back up.

Big Sausage, geez how he missed that guy. They used to have a lot of laughs together at their club, *L'Amici*—The Friends. That's what they were. Yeah, he missed almost everything about that place in those days. Being part of things. He missed the smell of garlic, the cups of espresso, maybe a small glass of rosso.

He would spend at least four hours a day there. In the summer they'd sit out back under the umbrellas and roll the balls. He didn't care so much about the bocce. What he liked best was the checkers and the fact that no one in the place could beat him unless he let them.

People had the wrong idea. His guys were thought to be a bunch of thugs who sat around all day dreaming up grave sites, dismemberments or chasing shopkeepers with baseball bats. Mostly, that was out of the movies. By the time Anthony came up, to a large degree, that stuff was history. If people really knew what it was like being part of their thing, they'd know it was mostly hard mental work thinking of angles. Sure there were handfuls of guys who still engaged in the rough stuff and they were necessary for the smooth operation, but those guys worried Anthony as much as they worried the regular stiffs. They preserved the image and kept the world on its toes but that stuff had never been Anthony's cup of tea.

Mostly he had been an honest businessman in an illegal business. Was that so bad? He didn't cheat nobody. He had games and machines and it wasn't his fault that the odds happened to always be in his favor. The people who played knew this walking in but they still played and some of them even won a few bucks.

He didn't run whores. He didn't peddle dope. He offered fortune-making opportunities and that was almost all. Maybe when he was a kid, he'd played a small part in some of the rougher sides of the business but he had to to get in. For him, in his neighborhood, it was the only way to rise above carrying a hod and slinging bricks, but he never relished it. He only did it because it was what you had to do to qualify. As soon as he made his bones, he began to specialize in what he did best and that was basically just manipulating numbers, understanding odds.

Don't get it wrong. There were certain advantages to being part of the thing. He never could have gotten his machines in all those bars if he wasn't part of it and he enjoyed that privilege. It kept a lot of people from slamming the door in his face. He also benefitted from people whispering to others about his membership. He enjoyed the comped tickets and the good tables. Of course he did. He wasn't Saint Francis of Assisi or nothing.

None of that mattered no more. He was out of it. He didn't need any more money. He'd hidden enough to pay for this Sunny Laurel dump until he died twice. He was covered. All that he hoped for was the acknowledgement from this jerk-off Little Sausage who maybe had missed showing up because he got stuck in traffic.

Christ, he was tired. He couldn't sleep good in this shithole. It didn't smell right. That was another thing he missed. Everything smelled like antiseptic, even the people who worked here. They were one hundred percent phony. They pretended to care if he was happy but he knew they really didn't. Why couldn't they say what they really thought? He missed that.

And why couldn't they turn up the frigging lights? Every single day it felt like the whole place was getting dimmer and dimmer and his eyes penetrated less and less. At the price he was paying they could afford to brighten this place. Were they trying to save on electricity?

Then there was the other problem. Actually, if he were being honest, it was the main problem. Even though he had relatively little to do with his own release from prison there were former associates who suspected that maybe it was a scam. Maybe the old guy had rolled over, they said. In case he was looking for fresh meat to feed to the Feds, as a group, it was considered wise to lessen communication with him. When Anthony sensed what was happening it was probably the most painful realization he had ever had.

Chapter 38

If he jumped out the window or stuck his head in the oven, the cops wouldn't have too much trouble determining a cause of death. It would be obvious suicide. Did he care? A good part of him wanted to make it quick and as painless as possible but if they ruled his death a suicide, insurance wouldn't pay out to Maria. The payout was the last thing he could do for his little girl. It did not really matter how otherwise he died as long as it was an accident and as long as it was fatal.

If he wanted to pull the perfect scam, he'd make it look like a murder. Make that prick across the hall be Suspect Numero Uno. How could he do this? Fuck it, he didn't have the energy to think it out.

Anthony struggled to stand. He used his walker to make it over to the closet where his best suit and laundered shirts hung. When he died, whenever and however that was, he needed to look good, even though it might not matter. It had been his intention to be buried in that suit so he'd look good. He needed to look like a man of honor, not some homeless wino. For his final roll he'd wear the suit. Should he go with the navy tie, look like a banker and not a gangster? That would require a little thought.

Chapter 39

Slumped in his chair, pistol next to him on his end table, Jack sat deep in thought. Life now was supposed to be easier, pleasurably relaxing. Now and again when he got too sentimental about the good old days—the glory days—it hit him. The glory days were really not all that glorious. They were filled with the anxiety of trying to meet deadlines, obtaining information in whatever narrow way was permitted, trying to succeed in the mission which meant always trying to gain sufficient evidence to charge a target. Mostly, it was about just trying to satisfy the bosses. There were a lot of bosses to satisfy. Whatever you gave them, they almost never were happy. That had been the worst of it for Jack. You could never breathe easy because it seemed impossible to push that boulder up the mountain.

It wasn't hard to remember the big days, that were capped by the televised takedowns, the perp walks, followed by the victory parties. Honestly, those were kind of few and far between. When he brushed aside the clouds of velvet, most of the job was sitting around in boring meetings where the guys with rank kept demanding results while making sure you stayed in line. It didn't get easier as a supervisor where you had to transfer the pressure and the demands to your guys. But it was better than this, wasn't it? He needed a goal.

He thought he had found a goal but that was thrown out the window when it was pointed out that his methods of finally being able to ruin the life of Anthony Finelli were, if not blatantly illegal, enough to get him evicted. Would that be a such a bad thing? He had to admit it would. There was no place he really wanted to go. The truth was, all of these assisted living places were probably pretty much the same and he wasn't sure he could take the hassle of moving again.

Finelli was up to something, but under the new constraints he'd never figure out what. The ultimatum was clear, anything that might antagonize Finelli could get him kicked out. He didn't know what he was going to do with himself now. All he had was … wait a minute! He still had his brain. He still had the training from the best investigative agency in the world and he knew a bad guy when he saw him.

Okay, so maybe he'd screwed up by harassing the greaseball but that shouldn't mean that the chase was over. He just needed to back off a little. Go covert.

As Jack's cloud lifted, Anthony's depression deepened. He had to admit that when he went to the mattresses against the guy across the hall he had come to understand that having an enemy was almost as good as having a friend. That jerk-off had provided an outlet for all his frustrations. Taking on a prick who was convinced Anthony was the embodiment of evil felt good. It made him forget, for a few minutes, all of his intangible losses which were becoming too numerous to quantify.

It was in his blood to chase a vendetta. Anthony was not a guy who always had a chip on his shoulder. He wasn't always looking for a fight. At the height of his career he did not swagger and challenge. He was happiest behind his cover as a small businessman. He wasn't the kind of guy who needed to break a bottle over the head of someone who disrespected him. Still, he didn't get where he was by being a pacifist. He never backed away from a fight. He really couldn't when he was climbing the ladder. Later, when he gained seniority, he had muscle working for him to act as his proxy.

When he was coming up there was one constant enemy: the Feds. He could build a church and sponsor an orphanage—neither of which he had actually done—it didn't matter, the Feds were always watching, always following, always listening and always hounding. When it came to Feds there was one cardinal rule. You could never hit back. If you did you gave them an excuse to press harder. The only move was to look impassive and make like you were unbothered. With cops, at least with the worst of them, you could always buy them. Play it right and you owned them. With the Feds, with a couple of rare exceptions, you just had to take it on the chin. To react was to invite the wrath of an army much bigger than your own.

Of course there were not-so-bad Feds among the herd of absolute pricks. There were guys who let you know it wasn't personal; guys who acknowledged that you were only doing your job and that they had to do theirs. But all his life they made it so he had to look over his shoulder, watch what he said because it was probably being

recorded. It was only natural to build up a wall of resentment.
Anthony might look like a cripple but he was pretty sure he could still take this guy across the hall. That's the way it looked until yesterday when suddenly, thanks to the word from the management to Maria, the battle was over with no victor declared. He couldn't recall feeling so disappointed. It would have been fun. It had taken his mind off his aches and pains. It had taken his mind off the fact that he was surrounded by milquetoasts. It was almost like the old days before things went so bad. He had to keep his eyes open, though. Maybe it wasn't over.

Though Jack had promised to refrain from further aggressive behavior against his Mafia neighbor it didn't mean he couldn't keep an eye on him. It wasn't what anyone would consider a difficult surveillance.

Maybe Finelli was hiding, either from law enforcement or other gangsters. Jack still believed that he had either an in-house contact who was acting as a runner or an external one who would come in from the outside delivering revenue, messages or contraband.

Finelli's contact could be anyone on staff from janitorial to administration. Or it could be that the person had yet to make an in-person meet. Jack had to remain open to all possibilities. When Finelli was in his apartment Hannigan had to be prepared to get to the door and to his peephole to spot any incoming visitors. When Finelli left his roost, Jack had to be out there to see if anyone made a pass. This could prove exhausting. With the guy alternately traveling by wheelchair and walker, it was trickier than it sounded. To follow the guy without tailgating was difficult. It reminded him of the days when they would track one of their targets down the turnpike. To detect surveillance the bad guy would slow to 15 mph in a 65 zone just to see who slowed down with him. In order to stay behind Finelli without tripping over him, Jack would practically have to crawl. That might draw a little more attention than he needed.

He would give the guy a fifty-yard head start before he initiated a tail. Then he would quietly start after him. Nothing much exciting happened until one Thursday. Finelli took an unexpected left when he should have gone right to get to the dining room.

Jack lost him and looked around and began to creep down the hall in the direction he had last seen him go. He almost fainted when

Finelli stepped out of an alcove in front of him.

"Jesus Christ!" Jack grabbed his heart. "You scared me to death."

"Maybe that wouldn't be such a bad thing. Why you following me?"

"What makes you think I'm following you?"

"What? You think you're smart? You think you're invisible. Every time I turn around you're there."

"It's a small place. Every time you turn around, everybody's there."

"Bullshit! I thought they told you to back off."

"They told you the same."

"And I did. If I was still going after you, you'd know it, ya prick bastid."

"Who you calling a prick bastard? You don't see me hiding in closets waiting for you to sneak up on me, do you?"

"It's not a closet. I should have you arrested for harassment."

"Me arrested? What a joke. I know who you are Finelli."

"You don't know shit, pally."

"Don't call me, pally, Finelli."

"What do you want me to call you? You're a washed up, crapped out fed. Hannigan, I know who *you* are."

"No you don't."

"Yes, I do. I remember hearing about you from before. You were not good at what you did then and you're much worse now!"

"I might be retired, but I can still do you."

"Yeah, well keep it up and see what happens."

"All you can do is eat, you fat piece of lard!"

In slow motion Anthony lunged at him. In equally slow motion, but just a hair faster, Jack successfully dodged him. Anthony would have lost his balance if there had not been a wall there to prop him up.

"Whattiya call that, dirtbag? Karate?" Jack gave a nasty grin.

"Just trying to get you the fuck out of my way you skinny old shit stain. Get lost before I hurt you."

"Forget it, hotshot. You can't shake me. Kind of sad, isn't it. You spend your whole life hiding from the Bureau. You think you find the perfect hole and here I am waiting for you."

"I'll tell you what's sad, you old douche bag. You're the one who's sad. You're fucking pitiful. If I was your kid I'd put you in a home. Oh, wait. He did, didn't he? Now get out of my way!"

"Or what? You'll rat me out to Miss Sally?"

"Maybe that's not a bad idea."

"Go ahead, let's see who's more credible. Me or the guy whose prison sentence included a charge of perjury."

Anthony maneuvered his walker so that the bottom of one of the front rollers landed on top of his opponent's toe. Jack yelped.

"Oh, sorry," Anthony feigned concern as he limped down the hall. "Did I hurt you?"

"Keep your eyes open, Finelli. I'm gonna be there when you make your big mistake."

Anthony released his grip on his walker and slapped his left inner forearm with his right palm, giving him a big *va fungul*, Italian style. Then he punched the elevator button, the doors popped opened and he boarded.

So now the greaseball was threatening to turn him in for harassment? He wouldn't dare. Back in the day they had to be careful because these lowlifes would run to their lawyers who ran to the courts claiming the FBI was up to dirty tricks even on the days that they weren't. Sometimes it worked. One of those guys even filed a Civil Rights complaint and an agent got transferred out to the farm league. Then there was that jerk in New York, Joe Colombo, who tried to start an anti-defamation league, but what had that got him? A bullet courtesy of Crazy Joe Gallo. Maybe it would be smart if he did back off, at least for a while. Before, when the Mob began to spot all their tricks, all the Bureau had to do was substitute some new faces, maybe put in some girl agents who they'd never recognize.

Jack had nothing. No solutions, but then he began to think. The object of this exercise was not just to make Finelli anxious. That was secondary. What he wanted to do was prove a point. The point was that Finelli was still active and probably using Sunny Laurel as a front. These guys were like sharks who would die if they stopped moving. Granted, Finelli looked like he would die even if he tried to keep moving, and soon, but Jack was still convinced it was a cover.

When he thought about it, following the guy every time he moved out of his apartment didn't accomplish much. First of all the guy didn't really go anywhere. He went from his crib to the dining room.

Sometimes when he was too tired to go back to his room, he stopped in the day room where the coots parked in front of the flat screen. He'd pretend to nod off but Jack was convinced that was part of the show.

On big days, he'd wheel his chair out to the garden and go down the path that led to that phony waterfall, smoke a cigar and fall asleep there until that girl of his or one of the attendants found him and wheeled him back in. So what was the point in putting a tail on him? He could accomplish the same thing by stationing himself by the window in the day room. From here he had a pretty good vantage point. He could see the guy come out of the elevator. He could watch him if he went to the dining room and see who might contact him there. He could watch him if he spoke with anyone in the lobby (which, so far, he never did) and through the window he could see him out by the waterfall. From here Jack even had a pretty good view of the parking lot where he could see who drove up either to meet Finelli or to leave a dead letter out in the thick bushes by the garden which was where Jack suspected Finelli conducted his business. So far nothing, but it didn't mean it hadn't happened or wasn't about to happen. Maybe the guy did his thing before Jack was out and about. That might be it. He had to start earlier.

By staking himself out in the day room at the crack of dawn, Hannigan came to learn of one of the little traditions practiced by the staff at Sunny Laurel. At least once a month and sometimes more often than that, a resident would be found dead in his or her room. The staff never talked about death, but given the age of the residents, they didn't have to. Some days there would be an empty chair at a dinner table, or an empty spot on the couch in the day room and you'd know that one of the residents had taken a permanent dive off the high board. No announcements were made and if a resident asked something like, "Whatever happened to Goldie, I don't see her anymore," they'd only get a vague response. Maybe it was because they didn't want their guests to become depressed or obsess that they'd be next. Maybe it was a privacy issue though it would seem that once you were dead all legal bets would be cancelled in the privacy department. Whatever the case, nothing was said.

Instead, if you happened to be out before anyone else, pre-breakfast, you couldn't help but notice all the staff quietly lining the hallway in advance of the covered stretcher being pushed down the hall and out to the parking lot. The staff, led by Sally, would follow the suited funeral home attendants as they pushed the gurney on its final voyage and stand respectfully on the veranda until the hearse pulled away. It was a quaint farewell. "You enter by the front door and you leave by the front door."

Jack came out to survey the parking lot first thing every morning about an hour before the first meal service since that seemed to be the most frequent time that the parade took place. Every morning, Jack would look out in the parking lot in search of the waiting meat wagon. He started his own tradition. If he saw the white station wagon in the circular driveway, he'd put his hand to his chest to check for a heartbeat, making sure it wasn't for him.

Most mornings after breakfast, Jack would perch on the couch on the far side of the day room waiting for Anthony to roll in. As often as not after breakfast, Finelli would navigate his way to the end of the day room farthest from Jack. Once situated, the gangster would look around, spot Jack and pretend to pick his nose and flick it in Hannigan's direction. In turn, Jack would cup his nuts then flip Anthony the bird. That was the extent of their discourse.

Chapter 40

They had decided to meet again at the Tropics Lounge, the bar which was conveniently located less than two blocks from Sunny Laurel. Both thought that another drink might offer the necessary relief after a weekend visit with their fathers. This was the week following their summons into the office by Sally.

Maria was seated in a booth. Michael came rushing in ten minutes after he had promised to be there.

"Oh, good," she said when she saw him approach. She plinked her wine glass. "I was thinking you couldn't make it. Maybe I can order another one."

"I'll get it for you and order a double Scotch for myself to catch up. I'm so sorry I was late. I got hung up with my Dad."

She gave him an understanding shrug. "Not a big deal. If I had figured out how therapeutic Chardonnay could be, I would have started this tradition a couple of months ago. Solo."

"I was trying to sneak around the front office so that Sally what's-her-name couldn't bawl me out about my father's conduct this week. Then as I made it through the front entrance, I ran into her coming from the other direction," Michael reported.

"And? Are we still on probation with her?"

"Surprisingly, she said Dad was doing fine. She thinks it's because she moved him to another table where he's distracted by making new friends."

"Huh. That's nice."

"Maybe, but I didn't get the sense that he's at all happy about his 'new friends'. Basically, and not surprisingly, he says they're a bunch of morons—not his exact words."

The waitress brought over their drinks. Michael took a sip, closed his eyes and sighed. "Heaven. How is your father?"

She shook her head. "Delusional. Now he thinks his phone's tapped or something."

"Uh-oh."

"Yeah and he claims someone called his lawyer back home impersonating him trying to get some dirt on him."

"Whoa."

"Yeah."

"Maybe there's something in the water over there," Michael said. "Today my dad kept trying to get me to see if I could find something called a reverse telephone directory online."

"What's that?"

"If a telephone number is listed, using one of these reverse directories you can look up a number and find out who the number belongs to."

"And that would be useful to him how?"

"Good question. The number he had was apparently unlisted so we weren't able to find out who it was registered to," he took another sip and burst out laughing. "Jesus, somebody could sell a book based on these crazy old guys." He glanced over at Maria who was staring into her drink. "I'm sorry. You don't think it's very funny, do you?"

"No, it kind of is, but I'm really worried about my father. He was practically hyperventilating he was so paranoid. He's never been like this before. I'm kind of scared."

Michael surprised himself by putting his hand on hers. "Really, I didn't mean to be insensitive. It's not easy watching them grow old."

"It's a definite role reversal. That's for sure. I just feel kind of helpless, that's all."

He nodded. "Maybe when you get home you can give him a call. Who knows, he might be over it by then. Look at how quickly and easily they gave up their grudge match. I don't know about your Dad, but mine didn't even bring your father up."

"That's true, but I think I preferred hearing how he hated *your* Dad to his current paranoid fantasy."

Chapter 41

Jack had heartburn. It must have been the meatloaf. The food here was usually so bland you couldn't taste it but they put in some pimentos or something in tonight's meal and he was getting stabbing pains in his gut. He could use a good dump, but that was probably not going to happen until the regular time which was about 0645 tomorrow morning, a time which had come and gone with its usual limited success. Christ! It was only 2230.

Another cramp hit him and he jumped up. He needed to walk, that used to work, but in this space he could only get about six paces before he hit a wall in either direction. Maybe he could run a lap around the parking lot. Or maybe he would just walk to the parking lot.

He put on his cardigan, then a zip-up jacket. Florida nights were a lot colder than it said in the brochures. He wondered if he should bring a flashlight. He didn't want to trip over an alligator or stumble on a python. He grabbed his flashlight just to make sure. It was his old five-battery Maglite, a police job. As good for goosing a suspect as it was for illumination.

He went downstairs and through the lobby. When he got as far as the benches along the parking lot, he decided to have a seat. A good belch, maybe even a small emission of gas should solve the problem. Then he heard an approaching siren. God, he missed that sound.

It was definitely approaching. Now he could see the flashing lights. Then the driver killed the siren and the ambulance pulled into the circular driveway. Uh-oh. Another one must have bitten the dust.

Two EMTs jumped out and put their first aid kit on top of a gurney which they wheeled into the lobby. They were met by one of the night attendants who led them to the elevator. Even with all the excitement he had experienced over the years Jack had never been able to just walk away and ignore when either a fire truck, a cruiser or an ambulance drove near his location. There was no way he wasn't going to stick around now.

Ten minutes later they were back downstairs wheeling the gurney. Trying not to appear to be a lookie-loo, Jack timed his return to the lobby to their departure. There was no procession by the

Sunny Laurel staff. Whoever was on the stretcher wasn't covered so he or she must still be breathing, but not by much. Whoever it was, the person was grey, the color of approaching death. He marveled how, once again, when someone was checking out as a stiff or a soon-to-be-cadaver you needed to really use your imagination to figure out who the person was. Part of the confusion was caused by the oxygen mask over the person's face.

The medics pushed the gurney by, just five feet from him and Jack still couldn't tell if it carried a man or a woman, but he knew from the looks on their faces that whoever it was probably didn't have a prayer. He hoped with all of his heart that it was one of the doofuses from his table and that the others wouldn't be far behind. This place would be considerably more tolerable if he could eat alone. The thought cheered him as did the fact that his exercise was sufficient to pass enough gas that his cramps subsided. He was ready for bed.

The almost dead guy wasn't one of his tablemates. He took a count at breakfast and all three of the doofuses were still there. The staff wasn't about to shed any light on the issue. They protected everyone's health crises to the point that no one ever knew who was up and who was down. They robbed the still-standing of one of the few pleasures left to them, namely knowing that while they might not feel tippy-top they were at least a few steps better off than the poor bastard who got hauled away in last night's ride to the medical center.

But Jack was a skilled observer and a trained investigator. His eyes danced around the breakfast room looking for an empty chair. There was only one and it belonged to Anthony Finelli. No way! He was sure he would have recognized Finelli on that stretcher last night. Maybe not. The guy was wearing an oxygen mask and all facial structure was lost to his illness, whatever that might have been.

He should have felt like doing a victory dance, but he didn't. He felt confused, but he wasn't sure why. He actually wasn't sure that Finelli was missing. Jack got up halfway through a moronic diatribe by LesCroates, leaving most of his scrambled eggs on his plate, which was unusual since the scrambled eggs were one of the few things he thought tasted halfway decent.

He rushed to the elevator and punched the button for the second floor. When he arrived he went down the hall and knocked on the door across from his room. There was no answer and no tell-tale rustling from within. He knocked harder just as Fernanda, the housekeeping supervisor, came down the hall in her usual fast waddle.

"That ain't your room, Mr. Hannigan."

"I know that."

"Yours is right across."

"Why the hell would I knock on my own door?"

"I dunno, Mr. Hannigan. Maybe you forgot your key."

"If I forgot my key, why would I knock on my own door? I'm the only one who lives there."

"I quit trying to figure out how you people think."

"Well, I'm looking for my, uh, friend. He missed breakfast."

"He gonna miss lunch and probly dinner, too."

"Why, what's wrong with him?"

"I'm in charge of housekeepin', not medical stuff."

"Is he alive?"

"Far's I know. Maybe you should direct your inquiry to Miss Sally."

Jack debated whether he should go back to the dining room and finish his eggs. Instead, he let himself in his room and slumped down in his easy chair.

That sonofabitch! He knew I was getting close. The bastard better not die before I close my case. Then he smiled. Only the good die young. He's probably faking it to get me off his tail.

Chapter 42

When your father is eighty-one, you don't expect good news during a hospital visit, but you pray that the news you receive will be gentle. When your father has been one of the primary focal points of your thirty-two years, and his health has been mostly stable, the thought of continuing life without him is, most immediately, inconceivable. She was met at the desk by a middle-aged physician.

"Miss …?"

"Yes."

"You are the daughter of Mr. Smith or is it Finelli?"

"Yes. Is … I don't know what to even ask."

"Well, thankfully the staff at Sunny Laurel found him just in time and they provided excellent measures to safeguard him until we got him here."

She let out a long sigh. "So he …?"

"We want to keep him here for forty-eight hours just to keep an eye on him during the period that things sometime go negative."

"Of course. That's great. So he's going to be okay?"

"Well, I'm afraid this is one of those good news-bad news moments."

"He's not going to be okay, then?"

"He was unconscious and hanging onto life by a thread, but we got him back to at least where he was. He will be able to return to the facility, but you know, given his age and fragility—he is not in the finest physical condition—if he's subjected to the slightest form of stress, this could definitely reoccur. In fact, at some point it will almost definitely reoccur and is likely to be fatal."

"Is there anything that we should do, I mean medically?"

"If he was fifty or even late sixties I would recommend a pacemaker, but I'm afraid that the surgery would be too much of a burden to his system. He will be more comfortable without it. Stated bluntly, he is a very old man and age means eventual death. His is coming, hopefully, later rather than sooner."

"So what have you told him?"

"The same thing I recommend that you tell him: he had an episode that wasn't fatal and a full recovery is certainly possible."

"Is it?"

The doctor shrugged. "It's as likely at this time as a complete relapse. Said relapse or collapse, if you will, may be just around the corner or miles away. The less his stress, the better his chances, so I don't think any bad news for him will be helpful. Efforts should be made to just, you know, keep him calm, relaxed."

"How do you make a man like my father less lonely?"

"I'm not sure."

"He's in an environment completely foreign to him without his people—without his culture."

"I can see how that would be debilitating and unfortunately completely outside of the realm of anything I am able to change. I can only help solve issues related to physical health. Mental health is not my field. You know him better than we do. I'm afraid what comes next is completely up to God."

She nodded.

"In the short contact I had with him, it was my impression that your father might be a bit confused?"

"How do you mean?"

"I mean it's likely or at least possible that his confusion and disorientation was brought on by losing consciousness and waking up here, but his responses were … unusual. He didn't seem to be sure of his name, for example, and there was some confusion about his, uh, life. Is that new?"

"Um, no. There are times lately when he seems a little delusional and that he believes someone is out to get him."

"Could be a form of dementia. I hope you can keep monitoring that."

"I will. But is there anything that can actually be done about it?"

"Not really. No."

It was Saturday. Michael showed up right on schedule. As he stood at his father's door, he couldn't help pausing before he knocked, trying to hear activity from Finelli's apartment. Maria was usually there for her visit before him and he hoped that she would show up for their weekly therapy meeting—that's what they called it—at the Tropics Cocktail Lounge.

"Hey, Dad. How you feeling?"

"Better than the slime bag across the hall."

"Mr. Smith?"

"*Finelli.*"

"What happened to him?"

"Don't know for sure but they wheeled him out of here two nights ago."

"Deceased?"

"At least at death's door. Not sure of the cause. The weirdos here aren't talking."

"Oh, no! Uh, Dad? You aren't responsible for it, are you?"

Jack gave a sly grin, "What are you talking about? What would I do?"

"I'm not sure. I just know that you two hated each other."

"Hate might be the wrong word. Let's just say we have, uh, professional differences. He's a crook. His job is to commit crime. My job is to …"

"Neutralize him."

Jack was thoughtful for a second. "Yeah, maybe. But not to kill him. That would be too easy. My job is to catch him dirty. That's the tricky part."

"But you're thrilled, right?"

"That he's dying or maybe dead? To be honest, I feel kind of disappointed—cheated. Let's go for a ride, kid. This dump depresses me."

Chapter 43

He took the final swallow of his Scotch, placed some cash on the table and stood to leave. He was halfway across the floor when Maria rushed in. He gave her a big smile.

"Wow, I didn't think you were coming."

"You were on your way out?"

"Yeah."

"You don't have to stay. I'll just have a quick drink on my own."

"Are you kidding? No, I'd love your company. Frankly, you look like you could use mine."

"That bad?"

"A little stressed maybe, but never bad. I'm happy to see you and would love if you could join me."

She pointed to the booth he'd just vacated and said, "Please."

They sat down, the waitress appeared and Maria ordered. "I'll have a Chardonnay."

"I'll just take a coke, this time."

After the waitress left he turned to Maria. "I just heard about your father. I'm so sorry. How's he doing?"

"What did you hear?"

"My father just knew that he was taken away in an ambulance. He didn't know why."

"He must have been delighted."

"Oddly, no. He said that wasn't the way it's supposed to end. Have you spoken to the doctor?"

"Yeah, of course."

"What did he tell you?"

"Not much to tell. He kind of alluded to the fact that this is probably the first in a short series that will end … in everything." She tried to fight it but tears begin to fall.

He took her hand. This time he did not let go and, he noted, she did not try to pull away. "I'm really sorry."

She sobbed. "It's not like it's a big surprise. He never took care of himself. Always ate the worst stuff. I mean I knew it was coming. He's eighty-one. I was just hoping … I don't know."

"What were you hoping for?"

"That, before it was over he would find some happiness, you

know?"

"I do know. I've hoped the same for my Dad. Instead, it just seems that no matter what, the last years are bitter and lonely."

She nodded. "Karma is a bitch, huh?"

"Karma?"

"Yeah, let's be honest. My father was no saint. He had an honest business but he also had a dishonest business, although he denied it."

"Even to you?"

"Yeah. Okay, we were surrounded by not so nice people. Gangsters, to be perfectly frank, but my father claims he ran the one honest enterprise in the family. Gambling. He said no one was ever cheated. Everybody got paid, because his games and his machines were straight. The only problem, and I'll grant you it's a problem, is that his entire operation was illegal. For all I know he was also involved in other rackets."

"You're saying your dad was actually a gangster?"

"Yes."

Michael burst out laughing.

"What's so funny?"

"I'm sorry. I'm not laughing at you. Or at him. I'm laughing at the fact that this is what my father had been claiming all along and I wrote it off as senility. It's so ironic. Really, I'm sorry. I don't mean to be insensitive."

"You're right. It's not funny. But he is my father. There's nothing I could do about it, but you have to understand that he treated me and my mother wonderfully. I even think, in his gambling business, he *was* honest. But I understand that whether his business was straight or not, there were, uh, employees whose job was to collect when people fell behind and it's fair to say that their collection methods were none too gentle."

"You probably never saw that part."

"My father claims *he* never saw that part. I never saw any part of anything. My father was very protective and I wasn't supposed to know. But my father was a crook—a mobster. He was completely connected. What they call a made man. Mafia."

He smiled. "Funny. I never thought of Smith as being an Italian name."

"Try Finelli."

Michael shook his head. "My God! So my father was right."

"Anthony Finelli. And he just got out of prison. They let him out because of his health. The government was always after him."

"The Bureau."

"Yeah and the IRS. He lived in fear, but believe it or not, he was a wonderful father."

"I believe it. Holy Christ. So my father didn't dream this up?"

"And you know, it seems I spent the better part of when I was younger, mostly as a teenager, dreaming for the day when he would be gone. It wasn't like I was abused. It was almost the opposite. He tried to give me everything. He spoiled me. But he always wanted me under his control, to protect me from stuff that I never had an interest in in the first place. Does that make sense?"

"Yeah. I'm afraid it makes perfect sense."

"It was like I was supposed to maintain this secret that didn't seem to be a secret from anybody—well, maybe my mother. She lived in a dreamworld. Everyone knew what my father was. In our neighborhood being a made guy was like being part of royalty, but he never talked about it at home. We all had to maintain this myth that he was just a small businessman, which he was, in part. He had a business that I suppose was legitimate, but the bread and butter came from a business that was definitely illegitimate, but which he took pride in running legitimately. That was what we were never supposed to talk about or even acknowledge, even though everyone knew about it and kind of honored him for it. From the dry cleaner to the butcher. People always gave us stuff for free. Everyone was scared of us, even though my father wasn't very scary, especially not to us. At school, kids used to talk about me behind my back, sometimes in awe, sometimes in disgust. No one would try anything with me or against me for fear that they would incur the wrath of the Mob. At the same time my father did all that he could to make sure I avoided his whole scene. To make sure that I avoided relationships with others involved in anything illegal. He would provide endless lectures about how he did what he did so that I wouldn't have to. He didn't want me to know any of his people. Maybe if I were a boy, it would have been different. Maybe he would have been less protective. He might have even have brought me into his business but I doubt it. I always walked around as if there were two thugs right behind me to take out anyone who tried anything with me. I think sometimes they were actually there. I never had any interest or intention of doing anything illegal. I just wanted to be away, you know? Out from under his over-protection. I wished for the day when he was gone and no one would know who I was. Now he's even a little bit crazy. Before he had this heart attack, he seemed to think your father was some kind of G-man who was out to get him."

Michael shook his head in slow-dawning amazement.

"What?" she asked.

"I can't believe it."

"What?"

"My father is a retired FBI agent."

"No!"

"From Philadelphia."

"Uh-oh."

"Who claimed that Anthony Finelli was the target of his squad."

"No!"

"Yep."

"My God. This is eerie."

"And everything you said about how your Dad raised you? I can actually relate."

"You're the son of an FBI agent!"

"Which is really no big deal. Except maybe now we can understand why those two don't get along so well. I thought my father was living a fantasy when he built up this thing about your dad. Could it be that in their past lives they knew each other?"

"Maybe. Your Dad could have been after my Dad like they claim. I can't believe it. An FBI agent right across the hall from a Mafioso! But I thought your father was some kind of executive."

"Not really. Eventually he made lower management, but if you are in the FBI, there is no bigger deal, at least to them. They see themselves as the elite of the elite, the guardians of the welfare of America. Frankly, many of the ones I've met are not so much. But in my house there was no higher calling. From as far back as I could remember, my Dad expected me to join the Bureau. He couldn't imagine me wanting to become anything other than a Special Agent in the Federal Bureau of Investigation. He made sure that there was nothing in my behavior or my background that could taint my future application—nothing that would in any way look bad in my background investigation. He watched who I associated with. He drove me toward academic excellence and made sure that my extracurricular activities would look good on my future application. It wasn't just my activities he worried about but my beliefs. He was trying to raise the ultimate Boy Scout.

"At the same time, I suppose not only was he trying to protect my future, he was making sure that nothing his son did would in any way hurt his reputation. Nothing worse than an agent who permits his own kid to get in trouble. The only problem with all of this was that I had absolutely no interest in becoming an FBI agent. Zero. I had met enough of them to know just how undynamic and unexciting these guys were or were permitted to be.

"Was he loving and was his heart in the right place? I never doubted it. We had some wonderful times as a family. But did I feel more than a little bit caged? Yes. Did I envy the kids whose parents let their kids express themselves and act out in the way kids do when they're growing up? Yeah, every minute of the day. And were there times when I looked forward to the day when he wouldn't be around to direct me? Most times. So yeah, I can definitely relate. But I was hoping that once he retired, he could shed that control, not just of me, but of himself and make friends outside of the Bureau. Finally let go of the paranoia, relax and enjoy life, but it doesn't look like there's a chance. He's ended up with nothing, just loneliness and enough overwhelming judgment to continue to make not just his, but my life miserable."

Michael's lips were trembling. He shook himself to try to shrug off the emotion. Now it was Maria who reached out.

He looked now at Maria. "You and I are supposed to hate each other."

She nodded. "I don't hate you, Michael. In fact, now I can see why we get along."

"Like the Montagues and the Capulets."

She smiled. "Kind of a nice way to put it." She squeezed his hand.

"Yeah. As long as it doesn't end the same."

Chapter 44

A hospital volunteer waited beside him in his wheelchair while Maria brought the car around. Anthony was able to stand, but with so much effort Maria wondered if he was well enough to be released. He needed some assistance to bend himself into the passenger seat of Maria's Prius. She helped him buckle his seatbelt before getting into the driver's seat.

She wasn't exactly sure how she act, but knew it was best to exude calm. "How you doing, Dad? You look great."

"Ah, you know. Tired."

"I'll bet. Well, there's a comfortable bed waiting for you."

"Yep." His voice was without affect. He looked straight ahead.

"Are you happy to be going home?"

"Home?"

"You know. Sunny Laurel."

"That's not my home, baby."

It was an argument that she didn't want to continue. "The doctor said they did a great job taking care of you before the ambulance came."

"What else did he say?"

"About what?"

"About what? Who are we talking about?"

"He said there was no damage done and that you're as good as before this happened."

"Liar."

"I'm not lying. That's what he said."

"Then he's the liar. I heard him talking to the nurse outside. He said that he was surprised I made it and that I might not next time."

"There doesn't have to be a next time, Daddy. He said you could live until one hundred and ten."

"Bullshit. I'm dying, Maria. I wished I had gone this time. I know what's next, it's soon and it might not be quick and easy. I could end up like your uncle."

"That's not so. What do you mean?"

"Coma. Pain. All of that."

"That could happen to any of us. Me, too."

"Yeah, but what are the chances? I don't want you to have to care for a vegetable. I didn't work all my life for you to get stuck with a bunch of stupid doctors' bills. I don't want to be a burden, sweetheart."

"You're not a burden. You will never be a burden."

"Not yet, maybe. But soon."

She tried not to sound angry, but her voice rose slightly. "Neither one of us knows what's coming, for either of us. What do you want, Daddy? What would give you pleasure?"

"I want to go back, Maria."

"We're going back. Now."

"I don't mean to assisted living."

"To Philadelphia? Maybe we could take a trip up there some weekend after you get your strength back."

"No. I don't want to go back there to the way it is now. I want to go back to the way it was when … before things went to hell. Before the stupid street wars started. To when we were a family and everything was happy."

"I would do anything if I had the power to recreate that world for you, but I can't. And by the way, I don't really recall those happy times. All I remember was you being worried, peeking out the curtains. Mom got sick she worried so much. Maybe we can find a way to make the most of what we have now. Admit it. At Sunny Laurel you can relax without looking over your shoulder. You're around a bunch of nice people—regular citizens."

"Regular citizens. I can't stand regular citizens. These are the dullest people on earth. They never have done anything. They haven't lived the life. They don't know, you know? We don't speak the same language. They might as well be frigging Chinese, honey."

She turned to him and he looked on the verge of crying.

"But at least you don't have to hide anymore, Daddy."

"You know what I really wish? I wish I'd never let them release me from prison. At least there I'd be with my own people, you know? Now they think I got cut loose because I made a deal. They don't even want to talk to me no more."

Her father was staring out the window, hoping she wouldn't see the tears.

Chapter 45

Michael studied his father as he sat on a bench in the garden. "You look worried, Dad."

"What do I have to be worried about?" he asked sarcastically. "Here I am in the Garden of Eden surrounded by a crowd of funsters."

"I would think you'd be feeling like a winner today."

"Yeah? Why's that?"

"Your neighbor almost died, thanks to you. He might still die."

"What do you mean, thanks to me?"

"He had a heart attack, Dad. According to the doctor, it was probably due to stress."

"How do you know this?"

"Let's just say I have sources."

It took Jack a few seconds to clear his mind. "Wait a minute, you're saying that the guy is still alive."

"He's coming home today."

Oddly, Jack brightened up, then looked concerned. "You're saying that somehow I'm responsible for his stress?"

"At least part of it, yeah. From what I heard, he got all revved up when you went after him."

"It takes two to tango, kid."

"Maybe, but if one tango partner doesn't play, if he becomes the bigger person and looks the other way, then there is no dance at all, is there?"

"You're saying I started it?"

"I'm guessing you did, yeah."

"Look, it was never my intention to do the guy physical harm. That's not the way we operate. That's not even the way they operate, at least not with us. I was doing what I'm sworn to do. Gather evidence. Period."

"You're retired, Dad. You are now being paid to relax."

"Hard to do when a big crook moves in across the hall, isn't it?"

"Maybe the big crook just wants to live his last days in peace."

"Not my fault if his guilty conscience is killing him."

"But it would be your fault if your pranks do."

"You care about this scumbag?"

"Not really, but I've gotten to know his daughter a little and she's a very nice girl. She only wants her Dad to live out his time gracefully, as do I with you, and this whole thing is tearing her up."

"You've talked to the girl?"

"Yeah, a little."

"Probably a gangster in training."

"No, Dad. She's a beautiful person. She just wants her father to have peace. She works in an art gallery."

"Don't tell me you like her?" Among the concerns upon which Jack obsessed was his suspicion that his son was gay. At this point if he even fell in love with a hooker drug addict he would see it as a blessing, as long as she was a bona fide member of the opposite sex.

"I like her. Maybe a lot."

"She got a record?"

"I seriously doubt it. She's a graduate of a Catholic women's college. Separated from her husband."

"Yeah? Any kids?"

"None. And she's really worried about the health of her father as I would be about you."

"Let me tell you something, Mikey. I don't believe that greaseball is clean. They never are, but it was never my intention to kill him or even physically hurt him unless he came at me. That's not the way the game is played, despite what you lawyer idiots might think. We play clean. Okay?"

"Promise?"

"Listen, Mr. Self-Righteous. We go by the rules. I don't need a newly minted lawyer to remind me of my oath of office which, by the way, included upholding the laws of the United States and defending the Constitution against all enemies foreign and domestic." He tried to keep from blushing having so recently—flagrantly (with the help of young Victor)—violated that oath.

"I just thought that maybe you considered the gentleman across the hall a domestic enemy and maybe you wanted to push him toward the end of his life."

"Never. Perish the thought, kiddo."

"Okay, the thought is perished but I would be really grateful if you just released whatever animosity you have for Mr. Finelli. He needs mercy at this point."

Well, Jack thought, maybe the kid wasn't a fag, but there was something wrong with him.

Chapter 46

They never spoke of it—their little two-man Watergate conspiracy. Victor kept it secret as if it were part of the test he had to complete before he could be considered a viable candidate for America's finest law enforcement agency. Jack also remained mute about it because he was frankly ashamed that he had engineered it.

But Victor dropped by whenever he had a break or a spare ten minutes to chat. Victor bled Jack for whatever information he was willing to provide about his twenty-five years in the Bureau. Perhaps out of guilt over their shared crime, Jack focused his discussions on ethical parables emphasizing that the key to a successful and satisfying career in the field was to live by the rules, to uphold the standard. He preached that a person who cheated or took shortcuts had no business in the business. Victor was a thirsty puppy, an eager acolyte. He lapped it up.

Jack had to admit, it eased his loneliness having a person who worshipped what he had done. It was nice to receive the young man's respect, but it wasn't quite enough. It was not close to the same as being able to share stories with a peer who had been on the street and had walked in danger.

Victor might never achieve his dream. It would be close to impossible for the kid to rise above the masses of young men and women who dreamed of joining the FBI because he did not, nor was he ever likely, to gain the education, experience or the necessary polish to be considered. Victor was a community college kid from a poor family who was unlikely to matriculate much higher. If he joined the military it was unlikely that he would ever qualify for a commission without a four year degree. He was a good kid though, and Jack would do his best to guide him.

Chapter 47

Across the hall, Anthony was too despondent to notice the frequent visits to his nemesis by the maintenance specialist. He had his own problems. He was surprised to wake up every morning. He didn't expect immediate death, but he did think slipping into a lengthy coma and becoming a vegetable was within the realm of possibility.

If he were to predict his future, he considered it highly likely that it would include a long-term coma. He had an uncle who had gone that way. Uncle Gino. The old man was half-dead for more time than Anthony had known him to be alive. His mother's brother had occupied the single bedroom on the third floor next to the attic doorway. At least a couple of times a week Anthony's mother would make him go up to Uncle Gino's room and sit there and tell him stories. The guy's eyes were half open, but he couldn't blink. The best he could do was slobber. There was never any response to Anthony from Gino. He just laid there for something like three years until, during the daily ritual of checking his pulse, there was none. Then off to Carapacci's Funeral Home and into the ground he went.

For some reason, that was how Anthony thought it would end— or rather, not end—for him. The next three years the most he could hope for was to become a smelly slobbering ball of cotton. He had carefully watched Uncle Gino just to see if there was anything pleasant about his coma. Did the old man have any fun while he lay there collecting bed sores? It didn't look like it. He just breathed, sort of. This wasn't one of those happy dream states. It looked more like a struggle, like Gino was trying to wake himself up.

If you were in an assisted living facility, the caretakers there would keep you alive. Once you slipped into a coma, they didn't send you home. It was a one-way trip. The care home people had a vested interest in keeping you alive: ka-ching! Your bill didn't go down because you couldn't hobble into the dining room no more and make stupid chit-chat. You were still charged at least the six large a month even though you couldn't shout "Bingo!" You were still taking up space and that was all the owners needed to continue billing your account. They didn't give a fuck. It just made their lives easier. Before long, if you had visitors at all there was an excellent chance they would quit coming. What for? There was no one really inside the shell there to talk to or give you credit for caring.

This wasn't the way that Anthony wanted to go out. It had been his goal to leave Maria a tidy nest egg and his blessing that she should live a comfortable life. If he slipped into slobbering dreamland, he'd be slowly but surely chewing up all of the money he had tucked away.

He was only slightly aware that his decline was of his own doing. His life had become without challenge, without stimuli. Beyond Maria, there was no one who understood, related, or cared. He was ready to die. He was just not ready to become a lingering vegetable. But he sensed it was imminent.

This nightmare consumed all of Anthony's thoughts, every minute of the day. While he waited, he fully expected to take a dizzy fall on the floor and slip into Zongoland. He looked out the window as a big truck went by.

Chapter 48

Jack was feeling claustrophobic. The window in his room didn't open and the air smelled like dirty socks, probably because he hadn't allowed his laundry to be done in a week. He was bored, more than usual. He hated daytime television and, for some reason, he couldn't concentrate these days on a book. The amusement he once got watching the stupid squirrel had run its course. While he used to enjoy jumping out of his chair whenever Finelli's door opened, the past week the only activity over there was generated by incoming people dressed in nurses' outfits. Finelli hadn't gone anywhere, not even to the dining room. Jack needed to get out, not to the common room where all the idiots were focused on *Fox News*, but outside.

He pulled on his cardigan and shuffled from his room to the elevator, down to the first floor, through the lobby and out to the garden. To his relief the area was empty. He chose a bench not by the waterfall where it was likely others might gather, but to one that looked out on the street. He sat down and reflected on how pitiful he must look. Like a bundled up old man on a bench in a park. Like the old Simon and Garfunkel song, "Bookends" which he had once found so sad and unrelatable. At least the guys in that song had each other. Here he was alone and it wasn't pretty but he had better get used to it. The sun felt good on his face. It made him drowsy. He must have drifted off because his head jerked forward then back. Why had he come out here? More importantly who just rolled slowly by on the sidewalk coughing. Couldn't have been Finelli. He hadn't left his room since he got out of the hospital. The sonofabitch in the chair looked like he was dead. Hey, maybe it *was* him.

Jack craned his neck. Nah, it couldn't be.

The guy pushed the wheels of his chair slowly and with great effort until he got out to the curb. There he sat, staring down the road at oncoming traffic. What was this? Was he waiting for someone? Why was he wearing a suit? Was he going to a wedding?

Jack lifted himself off the bench and went fifty feet behind Anthony, trying to stay out of his line of sight. Finelli, assuming it *was* Finelli, was focused on something down the street.

There was a stop light about sixty feet in the direction he was looking. The light turned green and the traffic started in his direction. The only oncoming vehicle was a big Walmart freight truck towing a long trailer. It started slowly from the light and began to build speed as it approached.

This was when it got weird. Finelli, or his corpse, leaned forward and with both arms, pushed on his wheels, as if he were trying to launch himself off the curb. But his left hand lost its corresponding grip, causing him to spin around in a full circle.

"Goddammit!" the old man wheezed, as the chair almost tipped over backwards.

Jesus Christ! It was Finelli!

Hannigan figured the whole thing out a second before Finelli's next thrust. A city bus pulled out as the signal flashed to green. The driver noted that the next bus stop which was just before Finelli's perch—was empty. He was concentrating on his rearview mirror, looking for clearance for a lane merge. He didn't notice Anthony move into a purposeful forward crouch. The old man had tightened his grip, this time on both wheels.

Anthony didn't notice Jack moving up behind him at a comparative run—comparative only because his effort was just a tad stronger than Finelli's. As the bus closed at an accelerating 18 mph, Anthony pushed his wheels off the curb, with all his strength, which happened to be a hair weaker than Jack who grabbed the upper back handles of the wheelchair, tipping him over on his side onto the concrete sidewalk.

Jack landed, somewhat painfully beside him. They found themselves staring at each other in confused shock from adjoining prone positions, still on the sidewalk as the bus thundered by.

"The hell you doing?" Jack yelled.

"Whattiya mean, the hell am *I* doing?"

"Just what I said, asshole!"

"I was trying to catch the bus. What's it look like?"

"You almost caught it right between the eyes."

"Ah, you don't know shit!"

"Yeah, well if you look that way, fruitcake, you'd see that that the bus stop is twenty yards up the street."

Jack slowly lifted himself to his knees and stayed in that position long enough to let a wave of dizziness pass. When that was accomplished, he raised his right foot until his knee was under his chin and with great effort pushed upward until his left foot was firmly planted. Once up, he righted the wheelchair, and pulled on its brake, to use it as a stationary post on which to lean.

Anthony watched this in stunned silence from his position, still fully prone.

"C'mon, you sack of garbage," Jack grumbled. "Get up before a car runs over your fat legs." He carefully placed both hands through Finelli's underarms. "Jesus, how much do you weigh? Use the strength God gave you."

"Get your fucking hands off me," he protested while leaning in for Jack's full support.

"Push up with your feet. Don't make me do all the work." He pulled and Anthony pushed and Jack managed to drop him clumsily in the seat of the chair.

"Whew!" Jack exhaled. "I've gotta sit down."

"Yeah? Well there's only room for one here," Anthony wheezed, trying to catch his own breath.

Jack shifted the brake of the chair into neutral and pushed Finelli towards the bus shelter.

"Where do you think you're taking me, asshole? You got a warrant?"

"I told you, I gotta sit down. The bus bench is the closest seat."

"Well, leave me here, dick-breath. I don't need no bench."

"Leave you here? So you could push yourself into traffic again? Like fun. I'm not risking my life for you twice."

"Then just leave me alone. It's none of your fucking business, Harrigan."

"Harrigan? It's Hannigan, you dumb bastard. You must have lost a few IQ points when you were in the hospital." He pushed him under the roof of the shelter before collapsing on the bench.

"IQ points? Do I look mental to you?"

"To be honest? Yes. You always did."

"Well, if I'm so fucking retarded, how come you never caught me?"

Hannigan was somehow reminded of the classic Willie Nelson song, "Lefty and Pancho," and he grinned. "It was out of kindness, I suppose."

"Yeah? Horseshit. You clowns don't know the meaning of kindness. You'd take out your crippled mother for a fucking statistic."

"And yet I just saved your life."

"More horseshit. You never saved nobody. And I'm the last guy you woulda saved, Hannigan. Who you kidding?"

"Even on your last legs, Finelli, you can't be honest."

"You calling me a liar, fuck-wad? I ran the most honest games in South Philly. You knew that."

"Maybe. Maybe not. Maybe you knew that the suckers would take their bets someplace else if you didn't pay 'em clean."

"You're a sour prick, you know that? You always have been. Even your guys used to tell us that on the QT."

Jack blinked. "What guys?"

"I will never give up a name, not even one of your own rat bastards. Even when I'm at the end."

"What do you mean, 'at the end'? We're all at the end."

"I might be a little closer to it than you."

"So you want to go out as a coward?"

Anthony's face turned red. "Who you calling a coward?"

Forgetting for the moment that it was less than three months ago that he almost ate his own gun, Jack said, "What, you giving up the fight?"

"What fight? Look over there at that fucking glorified nuthouse we live in. Does it feel to you like we're fighting any battles? We're done, pally. Done! I don't want to spend another day in that dump eating tapioca and listening to the bullshit of those pitiful assholes."

"Quit feeling sorry for yourself. You think you're the only guy in that place that can't stand it?"

"Maybe not, but at least you're surrounded by your own people."

"My own people? What are you talking about?"

"The place is filled with Mick assholes."

"I'll grant you the place is full of assholes, but no one says they're Irish."

"I say they're Irish."

"Just because they're not dagos doesn't mean they're Irish."

"Might as well be. I can't tell you how sick I am to be surrounded by them people."

"Guess what, *goombah*. So am I."

"Get outta here! You kidding?"

"I go nuts listening to them."

"Jeez, you too? You always look like you're loving it."

"It's my professional demeanor, the only thing I hate worse than listening to those goofballs is trying to talk to them." He got up with difficulty, grabbed the handles at the back of Finelli's chair and started pushing him.

"Where the hell you think you're going?"

"I'm taking you home."

"There? That ain't my home."

"I'm not driving you back to Philly."

"This is an unlawful arrest. You could go down for this, Hannigan!"

"Yeah, right. I'm not leaving you out here," Jack chuckled.

"What's so funny?"

"I was just thinking. I know you, Finelli. You're a piece of crap, but when it comes to covering your tracks, you're kind of slick. No, you're still playing some angle. You're up to something and you're afraid I'm gonna nail you."

"I been afraid of some guys in my life, but you ain't one of 'em. So don't kid yourself."

"Yeah? Blah, blah, blah."

"You're a prick, Hannigan."

"And you know what you are?"

He wheeled Anthony up to the front glass doors of Sunny Laurel, which opened automatically for them. They went into the lobby, past Sally Woznecky's office. She looked up curiously as the two passed in their slow, but mutually agitated state. Sally blinked, wondering if she was seeing things.

"I hate this fucking place," Anthony mumbled.

"Not as much as me," Jack growled.

"What do you know?"

"I know a scumbag when I see one."

"Look in the mirror."

Jack hit the button and pushed Finelli into the elevator. When the door opened on their floor, Anthony commanded. "Hurry up. I gotta take a leak."

"Get your key ready."

"Hurry!"

"Ah, do it in your diapers."

Anthony slid the key in its lock and threw the door open. He took over the command of his wheelchair and rolled it into the bathroom.

"You took forever. Now I gotta go," Jack complained

"Don't you have your own toilet?"

"I gotta go bad."

"So go at your place. I ain't stopping you."

"I might pee on your rug on the way out."

"Ah, Jesus. Then go ahead," he wheeled out of the way permitting entrance to his own toilet.

Jack hustled inside, closed the door, turned around and let loose. He flushed the toilet, washed his hands and came back out. "Now I feel better."

"Great. So get the fuck out."

"Gladly, you old colostomy bag."

"Yeah? Your face looks like a colostomy bag. A used one."

"You'd know, Finelli," Jack stomped out slamming the door. Then he grinned. For some reason this little interchange had been the most enjoyable exchange he'd had since he was admitted to Sunny Laurel. He couldn't figure out why.

Chapter 49

The next day Jack rode the elevator up to his floor after breakfast. The door opened and he found Anthony waiting, balancing on his walker. If he could have flipped his transport in the opposite direction, Anthony would have.

"Hey there, Sunshine. Still breathing, I see," Jack grinned.

"Fuck yourself, Hannigan."

"Going out to catch another bus?"

"Just mind your own business copper, and everything will be fine."

"I were you, I'd avoid the eggs Benedict this morning. The hollandaise is a little rancid."

"Everything down there tastes rancid, breakfast, lunch and dinner."

"No linguine with clams, huh?"

"You got that right. Now get out of the way so I can get on."

"Just making sure you're healthy."

"Whatta you care?"

"I need you to stay alive long enough for me to get a handle on your latest scam, Finelli."

"You could never get a handle on my old scams, what makes you think you can nail me now?"

"You're weak, that's why. You're falling apart. This is when you're going to make the big mistake. This is when I'm gonna take you down."

"I'm not so weak I can't still kick your ass, Hannigan."

"Yeah? Kick this, you guinea puke."

They both lunged at each other and missed, possibly intentionally, just as Sally Woznecky came out of a room two doors down. They straightened up and pretended that neither had just tried to kill the other.

"Well, good morning, gents. I can't tell you how nice it is to see you two hanging out together."

"Yeah, yeah, yeah," Finelli said as he boarded the elevator.

Chapter 50

Where was Victor? Maybe that dago jerk across the hall had flipped him. The AC in the room chilled Jack to the bone and he had it turned to the lowest setting. If he turned it off, the room became too stuffy. He couldn't breathe and then his sinuses jammed like traffic in the Lincoln Tunnel. He was wearing three sweaters.

Jack couldn't get warm. He looked outside. The blazing sun was frying the plants in the garden. That's where he needed to be.

Ten minutes later he was out on his bench across from the waterfall. Between the coolness of the mist and the heat of the sun he was starting to feel just right for the first time all day. He was even considering taking off one of his sweaters.

He perked his ears up as he heard someone approaching, rumble-thump, rumble-thump, rumble-thump. Jack turned his neck, at least to the degree that it freely swiveled. Who came crotchety-walking around the banana tree but Finelli, his fine self.

Without a word Finelli maneuvered his walker into park gear and eased his ass down to the bench beside Jack. A full minute passed before Hannigan spoke.

"I don't recall inviting you to join me."

"The way your mind works you probably don't recall much."

Jack thought about this and shrugged. He pointed to the pond fronting the artificial waterfall. "So what? Today you thinking about drowning yourself?"

"More like thinking about drowning somebody else."

"Do I need to remind you that threatening a federal officer is a serious crime?"

"No. That you don't need to remind me about. You and all your little Fed punk agents used to tell us about it every day we wanted to slap you for being such backstabbing pussies."

"Yeah? That's what you told each other, right? Musta made you feel tough."

"At least the city cops didn't give us cheap crap. When they did at least most of them were willing to duke it out with us like men."

"Be honest. Most of the city cops were in your pocket, Finelli. They were so bad the best arrest they could make was on phony charges."

"Speaking of phony charges, Hannigan, when you gonna indict

me, you talk so big?"

"Keep it on the QT, but the Grand Jury is probably meeting as we speak," he lied.

"Ah, horseshit. You got nothing."

Jack decided to take the game up a notch. "You never know, do you?"

"There's nothing to know!"

"You know why I'm glad I'm not a crook?"

"You'd never make it as a crook, Hannigan."

Jack ignored this thrust. "Yeah, I'm glad I'm not a crook because if I were a crook, every day I'd be worried. I'd be worried about who was going to roll over. Could be anyone trying to save himself decides to walk in, or call in, drop a dime, then cooperate. All it takes is one schmuck like that who's willing to add that missing piece upon which conspiracies are built. One little missing piece and we got a RICO or a CCE and all the key players go down. Or at least one."

Anthony stared at him. "You saying you guys got a new snitch?"

"Not saying anything."

"You just did, Shit-For-Brains. You just did."

"You're looking worried, Anthony."

"Think so? Think again."

"If I were you, I'd get a lawyer. Oh, wait, you already got one. Or maybe not. Maybe your mouthpiece rolled over to us. "

"I don't need no lawyer, Hannigan."

"Soon you will, wiseguy."

"We'll see."

"First of all: a— I ain't worried because I think you're full of shit and b— I kind of hope you're telling the truth for a change."

"Why's that?"

"How much worse can the joint be than this? Food would be about the same and the company would be a whole lot better."

"Easy to say."

"You're right. Easy to say for me because I been there. To be honest I didn't mind the penitentiary, you know?"

Jack looked at him. As far as he could see, the old man wasn't bluffing. Maybe he didn't care if he went back. If true, that kind of took the fun out of it.

When he got back to his room, Anthony dropped himself in the chair in front of his television, but he didn't turn it on. He suspected Hannigan had been bluffing, just trying to get under his skin, but the weird thing was, he hoped that he wasn't.

If he got indicted, there would be the usual move to lock him up pending trial as a danger to the community. What a joke! Even a first-year law student would have no trouble getting him out given Anthony's age and physical condition. They'd be able to string the trial along for maybe two years at which time the Government would lose half its witnesses, whoever they might be. And, during the process, they would go through a string of prosecutors who would leave the U.S. Attorney's Office for more lucrative pastures.

If Anthony was forty years old, he'd spit at Hannigan's feet and walk away. But the truth of it all was that going to jail these days had a certain ring to it. He could do the time standing on his head. Actually it would be a lot easier than standing on his head.

If he got lucky they'd send him to one of the old mob joints—maybe even Lewisburg again. He didn't want one of those country club joints in Florida or California. He never liked tennis and his golf swing was shot. Lewisburg would be just fine. He missed the seasons.

Here was the plan: Upon arrest he would refuse to cooperate with a lawyer. There'd be no one to argue that he wasn't a flight risk or danger to the community, nobody to argue that he was a good bail risk. He'd say, "Lock me up, cocksuckers, if you got the balls." If the jail was nasty he'd just fake chest pains and go to the hospital ward. No problem. While the Government dilly-dallied about trial strategy and the usual horseshit, he'd plead guilty before anyone could get in there and mess up the case.

Guilty! He'd *make* them send him up. At Lewisburg there were a bunch of former colleagues counting the days. The only days Anthony was counting were the days until he woke up not breathing. Maria would have no further expenses and she could finally start her life. It was the only way to go. For the first time since he's moved into Sunny Laurel he was at peace. He had a plan. Life was almost sweet.

The only remaining irritant was the prick Hannigan. Who the fuck did he think he was, trying to upset him and bring him down? He'd better come with an army. Anthony had to find a way to catch a little revenge against the Irish cocksucker. Then he found it.

Chapter 51

Jack had finally figured it out. If he got down to the dining room fifteen minutes before they stopped serving lunch there was a good chance his idiot tablemates would be gone and he would have the place to himself. Peace and quiet.

He sat down, thinking the hot roast beef sandwich smothered in gravy might be just the thing this afternoon. He spread the newspaper out in front of him, tucked the linen napkin under his chin, took a big sip of water (because he had found that there was a correlation between drinking water and a successful bowel movement), sat back and closed his eyes, waiting for the server to take his order.

"Hey, Hannigan. Wake up!"

Jack opened his eyes with a jerk. Finelli was balanced behind him on his walker. Jack frowned. "Ah, Sweet Jesus. You just ruined my lunch before I even got started."

"Good. Hey, you remember a guy named Salvatore Scarpone?"

"Squeegy?"

"He hated that name."

"I gave it to him because he was always in his driveway looking for surveillance cars while pretending to clean his windshield."

"He hated you."

"That's because I got him twenty in the penitentiary at Terre Haute when he should've gone down for like a dime. If he hadn't shot off his mouth about being a hitter he'd have done much less. He was dumb as a doorknob."

"But with a good memory. He never forgot you, Hannigan."

"Fine. He can dream about me in the joint. He wants to refresh his memory, I'll send him a picture. One of those selfies the kids are always taking."

"Maybe you can hand it to him in person. He's out."

"Squeegy Scarpone is out of the joint?"

"That's what I'm hearing. The word is he's heading to Florida."

"Bullshit. His parole officer would never let him leave Philly."

"He jumped parole."

"So what's that got to do with me?"

"He still hates you, Hannigan. Says you're the only thing he

thought about in the can."
"I'm not worried."
"Nah. You're a tough guy. Enjoy your lunch."
Suddenly Jack wasn't hungry.

Holy God, Squeegy Scarpone! He used to think about him all the time, but the gangster hadn't crossed his mind in years. Squeegy Scarpone had made Jack's career. If it hadn't been for Squeegy, Jack Hannigan would not have received his second Certificate of Achievement.

Squeegy was a notorious enforcer for the Philly Mob. He had been good for at least nine hits, though never convicted or even charged. By chance, Jack had stood behind him in a movie line outside the Hardesty Theatre in Philadelphia. *Rocky, Part III,* was the picture. Big thing back then—especially in Philly. Everybody had to see it. Every show was a sellout. Jack was supposed to be at work, but he took annual that day. In the ticket line a thug cut in front of him. Jack tapped him on the shoulder to get him to start moving toward the window. The thug spun around. Oh, Christ, it was Squeegy Scarpone! When the guy spun around a .38 fell out of his waistband. By the grace of God, Jack was quicker bending over than Squeegy, a known felon who now qualified to be charged as an Armed Career Criminal. The idiot.

Chapter 52

It was the end of another unsatisfying visit. Michael had made his usual Saturday trek to see his father. For him it was like going to Mass on Sunday—an obligation from which he derived neither peace nor joy.

He spent a considerable portion of his work week trying to mine topics of conversation he could initiate. They fell into two categories: 1) Stabbing at suggestions from which his father might discover sources of enrichment. He had yet to succeed. Or 2) Harmless topics that would not cause his father's blood pressure to spike. (Examples: the weather, things they did growing up, innocuous television shows.) Basically, he was seeking ways to fill the visit time in such a way that his father's mood kind of flatlined. Mood elevations presented anger and dives were the surest route to depression, so the best way to keep the old man in neutral was to come up with bland small talk. He was getting better at this but as often as not they sat around staring off into space wondering how long to extend the discomfort. It turned out that confining his visits to an hour and a half fulfilled all social obligations.

In the end, Jack would walk Michael to the front door, shake hands, execute a faux hug and wave goodbye.

To some extent a person's standing at Sunny Laurel was gauged by the number of personal visits he received. Michael wasn't certain that his father had any desire to achieve status, but it was important to Michael that there were witnesses to the fact that he was a caring son. At least when Jack retreated into the recesses of the facility, should he run into an inquiring guest or staff member, he could say, "That was my son, the lawyer." Maybe it was Michael who sought the status.

As they stood out on the sidewalk Michael exclaimed, "I almost forgot. I brought something for you. Let me get it out of the car."

"What is it?"

"A surprise, I think you'll love it. Just hold on for a sec."

"I'll go with you."

He followed Michael out to his new Jetta. "I don't know why you don't get a decent car."

"This is a decent car. Very economical. Diesel."

Jack rolled his eyes.

Michael unlocked his doors with the remote and reached into the passenger seat. He came up with an oblong box.

"What's this?"

"A checkers game."

"What for?"

"You used to love to play, remember?"

He remembered that when Michael was between eight and twelve, in an effort to bond with his son, every Sunday they would play the game. Usually, within about eleven moves Jack had the kid beat, even when he tried to lose. Michael, it seemed, had no interest in competition. More to the point he didn't care about the game. He'd look out the window or longingly at the TV and will the tournament to end.

"We used to love it, remember. Every Sunday."

"Uh, yeah."

"So I thought maybe we could play a game when I came over each week to pass the time."

"Did you keep the receipt?"

"Don't worry. It didn't cost much. We'll give a try."

"Yeah, great." He said with zero enthusiasm.

They did the quick handshake and the phony hug and both sighed with the usual relief that the visit was over.

Among the visions permanently tattooed to the brain of Jack Hannigan was the day that Squeegy Scarpone was sentenced in Federal Court in the Eastern District of Pennsylvania: Squeegy standing before the judge with his lawyer babbling on about how the case was a setup based on rumors of Squeegy's mob involvement and how the FBI sent in this guy Hannigan as an undercover to flake The Squeege—plant a gun on him—after he was lured to the theatre for that stupid Sylvester Stallone movie.

Squeegy, the mouth piece claimed, detested violence and could never have even sat through Rocky. Everyone knew that he preferred romantic comedies, and also had a soft spot for musicals. It was a setup, orchestrated by Hannigan, who the defendant had cause to believe, had even invented Mr. Scarpone's insulting nickname.

His Honor dismissed the lawyer's claims as irrelevant and sentenced the Squeege to twenty years in the can as an Armed

Career Criminal, followed by a ten-year term of supervised release. That was sweet, Hannigan reflected, but that wasn't the vision so deeply embedded in him. That came after the judge left the bench and while the Marshals reattached the ankle chains and waist restraints. It was during a pause when Jack was helping the Assistant U.S. Attorney bundle up his files that he looked up and saw Scarpone staring at him with the sickest looking smile on his face that Jack had ever seen. Grinning at him like he might grin at a thick piece of ribeye on a plate.

As the Marshals led him to the prisoners' elevator at the side of the courtroom, Scarpone gave Jack a nod and mouthed two words that didn't require particularly talented lip-reading,

"You're dead," he said without uttering a sound.

Jack's eyes widened. "Did you see that?" he asked the AUSA.

"See what?"

"The bastard just threatened to kill me."

"I didn't see a thing."

"He whispered it. That's a new crime— Threatening a Federal Officer. We should charge him!"

"I didn't see it."

"I did, that bastard."

"I wouldn't worry about it."

"I wouldn't either if I were you. It was me he threatened."

"Think about it, Hannigan. He just got twenty years in the slammer. I don't think you have to worry." With that the AUSA hustled on to the next courtroom for another case.

Jack worried about it all right. He remembered an older agent telling him once that you will probably get a million threats in your career, but somehow your gut knows when one is real. This one was real. Jack's gut knew.

Jack moved on to other cases. Over time, his memory became less fixated on the threat. Scarpone was doing time in a maximum-security federal penitentiary from which escape was impossible. Like so many of the most brutal killers, he didn't have a lot of friends, not even members of his own crew who, according to what Jack picked up on the street, didn't miss him much. In fact, some were as relieved as Jack. The hit man had no one who would do his bidding so Jack didn't have to worry about someone else coming after him. There were no threatening letters in between. Squeegy was down for twenty, which, during the earlier stages of that sentence, seemed like forever.

When was it that Squeegy took his fall? Hannigan did the math. It must have been around '02. What was that? Uh-oh, maybe ...

Being realistic, Squeegy would be what? He was at least a couple of years older than Jack. That would make him at least over eighty by now. Should he worry?

There were many prison stories about older crooks who managed to stay alive fueled only by dreams of revenge. Scarpone rightfully held Jack responsible for his case. What Jack regarded as his ultimate triumph could possibly come back to haunt him since it was unlikely that Scarpone had found God in the can. Apparently not, since Finelli suggested the guy had jumped parole and planned to come after him. But was the guy still capable? It was one of those questions you really couldn't answer until it happened.

Jesus, if it wasn't one thing it was another. Now he had to stay awake. It was clear that no one was going to protect him. He had to take care of himself. Might be a good time to clean the Glock.

As he thought about it he wondered, did he really care? He had mixed feelings. Maybe a bullet in the back of the head, care of Squeegy, wasn't so bad. It would solve a lot of problems and be so quick that he wouldn't feel a thing. Maybe that was the way to go. There was a sense of honor to it. It would wake up those do-nothings at the Orlando field office and avoid the inevitable—the inevitable being that before long they'd be sending in a caregiver to change his Depends every four hours and roll him over to prevent bed sores.

Yeah, Squeegy, bring it on, pal. Give it your best shot.

Chapter 53

That night at dinner Jack did something unusual. He waved down the food server and asked for a beer. You could get up to two alcoholic beverages—cheap wine or not particularly notable beer—per meal, lunch or dinner. Tonight, he felt like one—actually he felt like three or four, but one would do.

He slugged the beer down quickly. It went pretty good with the bland corned beef. This could become a habit. A little booze helped make this place look better. In fact, he might get his kid to make a liquor stop before the next visit: a six pack or two, maybe even a bottle of single malt. Why the hell not?

He skipped eating his salad. The beer made him want to pee. He stood up, in retrospect probably too quickly, left the dining room and hustled over to the elevator. He started to take deep breaths. He was dizzy. When had he become such a lightweight? What kind of Irishman was he that he couldn't handle so much as a beer?

He stood in the elevator with his back braced against the wall as it rose slowly to his floor. The door jerked open. He remembered seeing Finelli balancing on his walker, waiting to climb aboard. Jack took three steps forward until his right foot was out of the elevator and collapsed. Boom! Out cold.

He didn't know how long he was out. As he came to, he was aware that the blood had rushed to his head and someone was pounding the hell out of his chest. As he opened his eyes, he was conscious of Finelli crouched beside him, his walker tipped over by his side and the Italian was hitting him.

Jack waved his arms trying to interrupt the attack. "The heck you trying to pull?"

"You awake?"

"What's it look like?"

"It looked like you were on your way out."

"I'm not on my way out. Stop it. Get off me!"

"Quit yelling, asshole. I'm trying to give you CPR, don't ask me why."

"More like you were taking a cheap shot."

"What? Now you're going to charge me with Assaulting a Fed?"

"That's what it looks like from here."

"Then fuck you. Die. I don't give a shit!" Finelli pushed himself up from his knees, trying to get his feet under him. Then he raised his walker to a standing position and pulled himself up. He checked his watch as Jack pulled himself to his knees.

"Goddamnit. I only got ten minutes until they shut down dinner. What are they having tonight?"

"Corned beef. The cabbage tastes like coagulated vomit."

"Figures. Can you get out of my way, asshole?"

Jack limped away slowly down the hall. His head clearing. He held his chest. "Jesus. It feels like you broke a rib."

"I shoulda just left you there to die, you ungrateful prick."

"Maybe I wish you had. Hey, Finelli, do me a favor, don't mention this to that Woznecky woman or anyone else, okay?"

"What? Now you think I'm a rat?"

Jack paused before letting himself in his room. "Nope. I'm not saying that. A rat's something you've never been." He went in and let the door close behind him.

Anthony still standing at the elevator, allowed himself a smile and a nod.

Chapter 54

The next day Jack headed out of the dining room toward the elevator after breakfast. Behind him he heard the clop-clop-clop of a walker speeding to catch up. He held off before pushing the elevator button as Finelli approached from behind.

"Your heart still pumping, G-Man?"

"What's it look like to you, Finelli?"

"To me you look like friggin' Elliot Ness. Ten years after he died."

They boarded the elevator together.

"Well let me tell you. You look more like Edward G. Robinson than Al Pacino, scumbag. And at least I can walk without assistance."

"Not the last time I saw you. I been meaning to ask you whatever happened to that stupid grand jury? When the hell they gonna indict me. I need to plan my winter."

Jack thought for a minute. "Go ahead and plan it, big guy. It turns out they think you're too minor a figure to waste more government money on. I was told to keep an eye on you, though."

Finelli looked briefly disappointed, then grabbed his crotch. "Keep an eye on this, copper."

"Speaking of planning, what about that clown Scarpone? What's taking him so long? Is he walking to Florida?"

Anthony chuckled. "I was jerking your chain, copper. Turns out Scarpone had an accident."

"An accident?"

"Yeah, he fell off the fourth-floor tier at the joint in Terre Haute three years ago. Don't you got any sources of information?"

"I should have let you jump in front of that bus," Jack snarled.

"I'm surprised you didn't push me."

The elevator opened on their floor. Jack held the door to let Finelli limp out and they hobbled together down the hall, angrily pretending the other was not there. When they got to their respective doors, they both slid their keys in the locks after some fumbling.

Jack turned. "Hey, any chance you know how to play checkers, dirtbag?"

Finelli paused before answering. "I useta. I could probably remember."

"Maybe if I went real slow, I could teach you."

"Real slow? Whattiya take me for, a retard?"

Jack gave him a half-smile. "We'll see. Let's give it a try, if you don't have any heavy commitments this afternoon."

They stopped outside their respective doors.

Finelli stepped inside his apartment. "I gotta take a piss. Gimme ten minutes."

"I'll meet you outside. It's warmer out there."

As he buttoned his shirt in his bedroom, Michael gave the mirror over his bureau a little smile. "Man, if the old men knew, huh?"

From the bathroom, where she was brushing her hair, Maria spoke. "It would definitely bring on the next 'event' that cardiologist warned me about. But you know, I believe that it might give him some peace knowing that I had found a good stable man."

"Even an Irish one?"

"Admittedly, that's a problem. But you know I think he might say 'Whattiya gonna do? You gotta take the bad with the good.' Maybe it's your Dad we need to worry about."

"Yeah, it may take him a while to accept that I've slept with the enemy. Or the enemy's daughter who he thinks might be the family's bagman. At least he'd be able to say, "What the heck? At least my kid's not gay.""

Maria came out of the bathroom and put her arms around him. "Definitely not gay. Ready for another fun day at Sunny Laurel?"

"Ah, God, must all good things come to an end?"

She kissed him. "Maybe not. They could start again later, if you've got nothing better planned."

"There could be nothing better. What I'm thinking is that maybe it's time we quit worrying about them and start to think of ourselves."

Hannigan and Finelli sat across from each other at a picnic table in the garden. Jack opened the checkers box and unfolded the game board between them.

"It's much warmer out here." Jack said. "That AC in my room is out of control."

"You should call that Spic kid in Maintenance, whats-his-name?" Anthony suggested. "He's pretty good at fixing things."

"Yeah, we'll see. So, you played checkers before?"

"I dunno, maybe once or twice when I was a little kid, tell me the

rules."
"You want to be red or black."
"Don't matter."

They drove to Sunny Laurel in his Jetta. Maria looked at Michael. "Is this smart driving over together?"

"They won't know, I'm sure they're brooding up in their rooms. You go up first. I'll wait a few minutes before I knock on my Dad's door."

In the garden, Hannigan and Finelli wrapped up another game. "I think I'm getting the hang of this. It's kind of fun." Anthony said.

Jack couldn't understand why; Anthony had lost three games in a row. Even Mikey was a better player. He raised his eyebrows and gave Anthony a look which said he had just confirmed the Italian was a moron. "One more?"

"Got nothing better to do."

Michael parked his car in one of the guest spots, then came around to open Maria's door. When she got out, he kissed her. She kissed him back and then they both looked around quickly to make sure no one saw them.

Michael's gaze stopped when his eyes hit the garden and landed on Anthony in his wheelchair sitting across from his father, the checkerboard between them as Jack jumped three of Anthony's pieces in a row.

"This can't be happening!" Michael exclaimed. "Look."
Maria sucked in her breath, "Oh. My. God."

Jack had to admit, while beating Anthony was no challenge, there was something kind of special about taking down his old nemesis. "Maybe your just tired. That's the fourth time I took you out using the same simple strategy."

"Yeah, I don't know, Hannigan. I ain't used to playing anything unless a little cash is involved. It helps me focus. Whattiya say, copper? Half a buck a game?"

Jack's eyes twinkled. "It's your money, Hot Shot."
Anthony smiled.

The End

For your consideration, four hardboiled crime thrillers by

Timothy J. Lockhart

SMITH $15.95
"Smith — just Smith - is a tough as nails killer, a secret operative and tough fighter, and Timothy J. Lockhart makes this adventure a compelling must read." —Gary Lovisi, *Paperback Parade & Hardboiled* magazines

PIRATES $15.95
"... with bullets zinging and baddies converging from all sides, it's anyone's guess who will make it alive out of Lockhart's gruesome, exhilarating adventure." —Nicholas Litchfield, *Lancashire Post*

A CERTAIN MAN'S DAUGHTER $15.95
"...an enjoyable hardboiled read with snappy dialogue and a touch of humour." —Paul Burke, *Crime Fiction Lover*

UNLUCKY MONEY $15.95
"Lockhart's style is bare bones narrative. Just the facts in a linear investigation ... future Wendy Lu books will be quite interesting..."
—*Men Reading Books*

"Writer Timothy Lockhart delivers a straight forward, action thriller without frills." —*Pulp Fiction Reviews*

In trade paperback from:

Stark House Press, 1315 H Street, Eureka, CA 95501
greg@starkhousepress.com / www.StarkHousePress.com
Available from your local bookstore, or order direct via our website.

www.ingramcontent.com/pod-product-compliance
Lightning Source LLC
LaVergne TN
LVHW021821060526
838201LV00058B/3465